COURTSIDE CRUSH

VARSITY GIRLFRIENDS BOOK ONE

KAYLA TIRRELL

for A (so she doesn't get jealous that the last book was for J...)

"Two teams, both alike in dignity
In fair Marlow Junction, where we lay
    our scene
From basketball grudge to new mutiny
Where rival love makes rival schools
    unclean"

-Probably not Shakespeare

CHAPTER ONE

BARELY OVER A MONTH into the school year and I was already in trouble.

I sat on a small plastic chair outside of the principal's office while my parents talked with Mr. Richards behind the closed door. My eyes followed the ugly swirls of green and purple on the outdated carpet of the school office as I waited to be called inside. While I couldn't make out the words that were being exchanged, I could hear the exasperation in my mother's voice. The frustration in my father's tone was undeniable.

Couldn't they see that I was the victim here?

Earlier that day, I'd caught my boyfriend, Anderson, making out with one of the cheerleaders under the bleachers when he was supposed to be eating lunch with me. When he didn't take his usual seat next to me in the cafeteria, I'd gotten worried. I raced through the halls in search of him, only to discover his tongue halfway down another girl's throat.

Who could have predicted that when I accidentally bumped into his car after lunch with my keys in hand, that the words "cheating scumbag" would somehow become etched into the side of his door?

Unfortunately, Linzie—the cheerleader in question—caught me in the act, and even managed to record me on her phone. Soon, the video found its way to the administration of Rosemark High.

I'd been called up to the office, classwork in hand, and had spent the rest of the day hanging out with the secretary. Since both of my parents worked, I was forced to stay there until they could come get me. I looked over the same worksheet about twenty times since my cell phone had been confiscated the first time I pulled it out.

I hated having so much time to my thoughts because they inevitably kept going back to Anderson. We'd been dating for several months, and while I didn't have delusions about forever with him, I thought we'd keep dating until graduation. Or at least until the Homecoming dance in a few weeks.

All the while, he'd been making eyes at Linzie! I wondered how long it had been going on behind my back, and if Linzie was the only one. Yeah, Anderson was hot, and he could be a jerk sometimes, but I thought he had at least one shred of decency.

My stomach churned as I thought about how he and

Linzie spent the rest of the day while I spent my time getting dirty looks from the secretary these last few hours.

The sound of Mr. Richards' door squeaking as it opened caused me to look up. "Care to come in and have a seat?" he asked when my eyes met his.

I was upset enough that I almost said no, but it wasn't really a question, and we both knew that. Reluctantly, I got up from my post and followed my principal into the office dragging my backpack on the ground behind me.

He shut the door as I plopped myself down beside Mom. Mr. Richards took a seat behind his desk and steepled his hands in front of his face. He peered at me over the thick frames of his glasses.

"Miss Royce, your parents and I have been discussing your behavior earlier today—more specifically, what you did to Anderson Webb's car."

I turned to them and opened my mouth to defend myself.

Mom shook her head. "Charlie, not now."

"Dad," I pleaded. My eyes were wide begging him to understand.

He lifted his hand and let out a deep sigh. "We've spent so much time in Mr. Richards' office these past several years, your mother and I have practically earned our own parking spot. We've been easy on you. We've let you get away with too much, I know. But keying Anderson's car?"

"He cheated on me!"

"That doesn't make it okay to destroy his car," Mom argued.

"Well, now everyone knows to stay away from him. If you think about it, I'm really doing the girls of Rosemark, and surrounding schools, a favor." I tucked a loose strand of brown hair that had fallen loose from my ponytail behind my ear.

Mom sighed and rubbed her temples with both hands. "Charlie."

I leaned back in my chair and crossed my arms—just barely resisting the urge to roll my eyes.

When Mr. Richards cleared his throat, we all turned to look at him. "As I said, we've been discussing what transpired earlier today, and I've recommended Saturday work detail for the next eight weeks. There's a group called Marlowe Junction's Helping Hands that takes troubled youth to clean up parks and do other community service projects around town."

I sat back up. "Troubled youth? That's not me. I got upset and scratched up Anderson's car, but I am not some kind of delinquent."

No one said anything. My parents refused to meet my panicked eyes.

"Mom? Dad?"

They'd always put up with my antics, but this meeting was different. The sudden change in atmosphere made me anxious. My heart pounded in my chest as a real sense of fear overcame me. What was going on?

Mr. Richards spoke up again. "It's not really a suggestion at this point, but a requirement." He let loose a long breath. "If you fail to comply with the community service hours, I'll have no choice but to expel you from Rosemark."

"Expel me?" My heart dropped into my stomach. "What would I do? How would I finish school?"

My dad answered me, his voice soft. "You'd finish out your year at Hope for the Future Academy."

"Juvie?" I cried. "You've got to be kidding me!"

"Charlie." My dad's voice was soothing. "It's not juvie, it's an alternative school for at-risk teens."

"But I'm not at risk," I pointed out. "I don't drink, I don't smoke. I get good grades."

"It's more than what your report card says." My dad turned his attention to my principal once again, and I had no choice but to follow his lead.

"Your behavior over the last three years has gone unpunished for too long." Mr. Richards opened up the folder in front of him and began to read. "Freshman year, you started no less than two food fights in the cafeteria."

The first time it happened was because one of the cheerleaders had made some horrible comment about my brother and his red hair, likening him to a certain fast-food restaurant mascot. I had to do something.

The second time was much less justified. It only started because I refused to back down after my best friend, Daria, dared me to try to hit one of the theater kids whose very loud monologue had gone on long enough.

But everyone had gotten in on it, and we all had to stay and clean the mess up. It was unfair to single me out and punish me twice. I was just about to tell Mr. Richards as much when he continued.

"Sophomore year, you cut the hair of three cheerleaders during a school assembly."

Again, because they were being absolutely wretched people, spreading nasty rumors this time.

"It grew back," I argued, but couldn't stop the upward tilt of my lips as I remembered their reactions.

Mom shushed me.

Mr. Richards fixed me with a stare. "Junior year, you were caught running a black-market on test answers for biology."

"Public service."

Those tests were hard, and we all would have failed without them. Once I'd gotten caught, everyone started getting F's. The next year, there was a significant shift in the science department—or more accurately, it was down one biology teacher who almost failed the entire junior class.

"Which brings us to senior year when you keyed Mr. Webb's car just a few weeks into the school year."

"Allegedly."

Mr. Richards closed his eyes. "This is not the criminal court system, Miss Royce. You're not innocent until proven guilty. Not to mention there's footage of you doing it."

"But—"

"We're not even including your countless dress code violations and excessive tardiness." Mr. Richards paused and ran his hand over the thin patch of gray hair that covered the top of his head. "I should have done this years ago, but kept thinking you would eventually grow up. However, it doesn't look like that's going to happen without some serious consequences."

"We've laid out this student/parent contract for you and your parents to sign," Mr. Richards continued as he slid a piece of paper across his desk toward me. I quickly looked it over. It basically said what he'd just told me. I was required to fulfill a set number of community service hours each Saturday with Marlowe Junction's Helping Hands for the next eight weeks. Failure to comply would mean my immediate expulsion from Rosemark High.

I stared at the paper in silence, feeling the weight of everyone's eyes on me. It was only eight weeks, but I could still feel the sting of tears in my eyes. I blinked quickly several times to stop them from falling. There was a pen on the top of the desk, and my hands shook as I reached for it.

Mom squeezed my shoulder, and I closed my eyes. There was no choice here. Either I signed the paper and picked up trash on the side of the road, or I ended up in some school full of kids who were seriously bad news.

I wouldn't survive two weeks in a place like that, I just knew it.

I sighed and quickly scribbled my name at the bottom of the contract. When I finished, I slid the paper and pen toward Mom. She did the same, and soon it was in my dad's hands. Surprisingly, he took the longest of the three of us. He looked up at Mr. Richards who nodded his head at him. My dad hesitated but, eventually, he signed as well.

When the contract returned to Mr. Richards, he added his name without a second of hesitation. "Well, then it's settled. Miss Royce, your first work detail is tomorrow. Mrs. Gibbs, the director of Helping Hands, was kind enough to fax over some papers about what to expect."

He handed me a stack of papers. I folded them, not bothering to read them in front of everyone, and held them with both hands in front of me.

My parents stood up from their seats and stuck their hands out to shake my principal's hand. "Thank you, Mr. Richards."

Mom looked down at where I still sat in my chair and raised her brows. Feeling sick, I got up from my seat and reached out to shake Mr. Richards' hand. "Thanks," I mumbled under my breath.

Although, for the life of me, I couldn't imagine what I was thanking him for.

Thank you, Mr. Richards, for always having it out for me. Thank you for calling my parents to your office. Thank you for eight weeks of community service.

Oh, what would I do without a loving and caring principal such as yourself?

I slung my backpack over my shoulder.

"Oh, and one more thing, Miss Royce." I stopped and turned on my heel to face my principal. "Until you complete your eight weeks with Helping Hands, consider yourself on athletic probation."

My heart stopped in my chest. "What?"

That was almost worse than the possibility of getting

expelled. Basketball was my life, and hopefully my ticket to college. How was I supposed to impress college scouts and get the scholarship I'd been counting on if I couldn't play?

My tears fought hard to fall once more, but I fought harder. I bit the inside of my cheek as I gave him a tight smile. So hard, in fact, I tasted the copper tang of blood as my teeth cut the sensitive tissue. I walked out of his office without another word.

I followed my parents past the secretary. She smiled at Mom and Dad but was sure to give me one last frown as I passed by her desk, almost "forgetting" to give me my phone back on the way out.

The three of us walked out of the building in silence, to where their run-down SUV was parked in a visitor spot. We all piled in, and once everyone was settled, my mother started talking.

"What were you thinking, Charlie?"

"Anderson was making out with Linzie. What was I supposed to do?"

"I don't know, Charlie," my dad answered. "Maybe not write 'cheating scumbag' on his car? You really did a number on it."

"And yet no one seems to care that he destroyed my heart, do they?" I slammed back against my seat blinking back tears. Since when was a boy's car considered more important than a girl's broken heart?

"Don't be so dramatic," Mom gently chided. "You two have only been dating for a few months."

Six months, one week, and two days, to be exact. It felt like a lot more than just a "few months" to me.

"Am I not allowed to be upset?"

"Of course you are, Charlie." My dad turned in his seat to look directly at me. "No one is saying you can't be upset. If I'm being transparent here, I'm pretty angry myself. Anderson should have at least had the decency to break up with you before moving on to that Linzie girl."

I snorted. "Gee, thanks."

"You know what I mean. I'm not happy about what Anderson did to my baby girl, but I'm also disappointed to hear how you reacted. Haven't your mother and I taught you to be the bigger person? Haven't we raised you to know better than that?"

My cheeks heated as I let his words sink in. I hated letting him down. "I'm sorry."

My dad searched my face. "I know you are."

"Then does that mean I don't have to go through with Saturday work detail?" I asked, my voice hopeful.

A small smile touched my dad's lips as he shook his head. "It's not that simple. We all signed that contract."

"There's no way it's legally binding. I was forced to sign under duress."

His smile grew. "The contract stands. And besides, maybe it will be good for you to have some repercussions. Strike some fear into your heart."

My mom turned around in her seat and looked at me. The traces of anger had disappeared from her face. "Your father's right. Sometimes tough love is the best way to love your children. We don't want to see you get yourself into a mess you can't get out of."

"Yeah, okay," I said quietly and closed my eyes. But it wasn't okay. Everything had gone completely sideways in a matter of hours.

Soon, the car engine started, and my dad began the drive home. Once I was sure they wouldn't try to engage in any more conversation, I put in my earbuds, and started playing some music.

Then, it was time to get started on the five-million texts that lit up my screen. Everyone wanted to know what happened, including my brother, Pres. I ignored most of them, choosing only to respond to two people.

First, my best friend and the most amazing center on the basketball team, Daria, who had messaged me right after lunch.

1:03 *PM*

Daria: Someone said Anderson was making out with Linzie?! And that you had to go to the principal's office? Is that where you've been hiding out since lunch?

Charlie: Yep.

Daria: What did Mr. Richards say?

Charlie: Long story. I'll call you later.

Daria: That bad?

Charlie: You have NO idea...

Daria: I want ALL the details. Seriously.

Charlie: Okay. But not right now.

And then there was Anderson, devil-incarnate. His message came a little later than Daria's.

1:34 PM
Anderson: WTF!! CHARLIE! MY PARENTS ARE GOING TO KILL ME!
Charlie: Maybe you should have thought about that before going and getting herpes from Linzie.
Anderson: It was a KISS!
Charlie: Because that's soooo much better???
Anderson: And there you go being a psycho again.
Charlie: Oh, right. Because *I'm* the one in the wrong here.
Anderson: You KEYED my car!!!!!!!!
Charlie: You made out with Linzie!!!!!!
Anderson: You're right. And it was so much better than kissing you. I should have broken up with you weeks ago.
Charlie: I wish you had!
Anderson: Have fun going to Homecoming without me. Maybe some band-geek will take pity on you and let you tag along. But I bet you end up going alone like a loser.

A growl erupted in the back of my throat. I was angry, I was hurt, and I didn't know how to handle such overpowering emotions in the back of my parents' vehicle. I turned my phone's screen off as I wiped a rebellious tear from my left eye and ignored the rest of the messages that came from him or anyone else.

I listened to the heavy beats that were blaring straight to my eardrums, not really enjoying the music that usually cheered me up. As my dad pulled up to our home, I saw Preston shooting hoops out front. The honk of the car's horn caused him to pause and stand to the side. He held the basketball under his arm as he watched the vehicle pull into the garage.

My dad and mom quickly got out of the SUV and walked inside. I lingered outside and walked over to where my brother stood once they were safely in the house. Preston was breathing heavily, and his bright red hair was plastered to his forehead from sweating so much.

He'd been practicing hard all summer for basketball season, with one single purpose—destroy Brooks.

Brooks was a player on Pinebrook's varsity team, and he and my brother had a history of fouling each other on the court. Whenever our schools played, they were on each other like white on rice. It was almost unhealthy the way those two had it out for one another. But when Brooks had caused Pres to miss the game-winning shot last year, the rivalry had turned into a full-blown obsession.

I sighed and tipped my head at the basketball tucked under my brother's arm.

"Practicing for the Senior Year Rematch?"

"Uh, yeah," he admitted, a slight blush hitting his cheeks. He shook his head and changed the subject. "But that's not important right now. What happened with Anderson?"

I shrugged. "He was kissing one of the cheerleaders, so I keyed his car."

"You're crazy."

"And he's a complete tool." I set my backpack on the pavement.

"No argument there. Honestly, I don't know that I'd talk to him if he wasn't one of the best players on the team." He paused and then jerked his chin at me. "So what did Mr. Richards say?"

"I have to do eight weeks of community service, or he's going to expel me." I looked down at my shoes.

"Wait? They threatened to kick you out of Rosemark?"

I nodded and looked back up. "Even made me sign a contract."

"That's rough, Charlie."

"That's not even the worst part. I'm on athletic probation until I finish it."

Preston's eyes went wide. "What about tryouts?"

"I know." I shook my head.

"You're practically a shoo-in for captain."

"I know," I repeated. "But what am I supposed to do? Linzie had footage of me scratching Anderson's car. My hands were tied."

Preston whistled low.

We stood in silence for several moments, before my brother started bouncing the basketball in front of him. "Wanna play a little one-on-one?"

I smiled.

Even though Preston and I were not related by blood,

he knew me better than anyone else. Our parents had met when we were both in first grade. My dad and his mom fell in love, got married, and the two of us became siblings overnight. We were young enough that we struggled to remember what it was like before we became a family.

And because of our close relationship, Preston knew I didn't want to talk right now. Getting my frustration out on the court—or in this case, our driveway—was precisely what I needed.

Sure, there'd be a time for tears over the phone with Daria, and I knew there was a gallon of chocolate ice cream in the freezer with my name on it. But, in the meantime, a little friendly competition was better than either of those.

I got into a defensive stance. "Oh, you're on."

CHAPTER TWO

MY PHONE BUZZED OBNOXIOUSLY as my Saturday morning alarm roused me from my sleep. It was 7:30 AM. I should have still been sleeping, not getting ready to go work at the local park. The sun was just coming up over the horizon, and there were still precious moments before the day actually started.

I silently cursed Anderson, Linzie, Mr. Richards, and anyone else I could think of as I crawled out of bed and looked at the papers from Marlowe Junction's Helping Hands.

Mrs. Gibbs, the director, outlined the next eight weeks with remarkable detail. From where it was, to what to wear, Mrs. Gibbs had obligatory volunteer hours down to a science.

This Saturday and next were spent picking up trash and working on "beautification" at Saunders Park. The instructions said to wear comfortable clothing, tennis shoes, a hat, and sunscreen.

I put on an old tee-shirt for some local band I didn't listen to anymore, some work-out shorts, and my favorite worn-out Chucks. When I finished getting dressed, I gathered my shoulder-length locks into a ponytail before slipping it through the back of one of my baseball hats. It had the word NOPE on it in all block letters and summed up how I felt that morning.

Nope, I didn't want to be awake.

Nope, I didn't want to clean up trash.

And, nope, I didn't want to do this for eight weeks.

As I walked down the hall past my brother's room, I was tempted to pound on the door out of spite but forced my hands at my sides as I made my way to the kitchen. I wasn't really mad at Preston, even though he got to sleep in while I was forced to go volunteer. It wasn't Preston's fault Anderson was a jerk and that all of this horrible junk had happened to me.

I just wasn't convinced it was entirely mine either, and *that* made me grumpy toward everyone.

When I entered our kitchen, I saw my mom sitting at the small table in the corner. Her red hair was piled on top of her head in a messy bun. She wore a green robe that was wrapped around her tight as she read the paper.

"Hey, Mom," I said tentatively as I walked in.

"Good morning, Charlie." She smiled as she got up from her seat. "I thought I could make you breakfast before your Saturday work detail. What do you think?"

I looked down at my phone. I'd been cutting it close with setting my alarm so late. "I can't. I gotta be there in fifteen minutes."

"Oh, okay." Disappointment marred her features, but she quickly turned toward the cabinet and pulled down a granola bar.

After yesterday's visit to the principal's office, I was surprised she'd want to eat with me. If I had known, I might have woken up a few minutes earlier.

"Here," she said, sticking out the sad excuse for breakfast. "At least take this, so you have something in your belly before you go."

I reached out and grabbed the food from her. "Thanks."

"Good luck today."

"Thanks, Mom," I said as I grabbed the keys to the car Pres and I shared.

But it wasn't luck I needed. I wasn't off for a job interview or even a basketball game. I was picking up garbage at Saunders Park. The task was so menial, I could do it with my eyes closed. No, what I needed to make it through the day was a whole lot of patience.

I PULLED up to Saunders Park ten minutes later.

There was a small group of kids gathered around a stern, heavy-set woman I could only assume was the director. She was already barking out orders as I walked over.

"You must be Charlotte Royce."

"Charlie," I corrected.

"Well, *Charlie*," she said putting an emphasis, that sounded a lot like mocking, on my name. "Welcome to Helping Hands. I'm Mrs. Gibbs, and we were just discussing this morning's duties. It looks like you'll be in the north quadrant today."

She put a large, black bag in one of my hands and a pole with a metal spike on the end in the other. Then, she pointed to where I was supposed to go.

My gaze went to my assigned area and I saw that not only was the "north quadrant" less shaded than the rest of the park, it also appeared to be much messier. I turned back to face Mrs. Gibbs who watched me with a look that begged me to argue.

I took a deep breath and gave her a tight smile. As much as I wanted to argue, it wasn't going to do me any good. I needed to make it through these next weeks without making things worse.

But that didn't mean I had to be happy about it.

I stomped off to my assigned area grumbling under my breath the entire way. Once there, I stabbed the first piece of trash—a hamburger wrapper—and lifted it to the opening of the bag. With it safely inside, I poked the next thing and also dropped it inside the bag. I did this with the next piece, and the next, and the next.

No one joined me in my quadrant, but it was okay because soon I was actually searching for the biggest pieces of trash in my area. Turned out, picking up trash was quite therapeutic if you went into it with the right attitude. And the right attitude consisted of lots and *lots* of angry jabbing and cursing.

"Stupid..." I slammed the pole into a paper cup.

"Anderson..." This time a napkin.

"And his stupid..." A piece of cardboard.

"Mouth."

I saw a large plastic soda bottle begging to have a spike jammed through its side and smiled to myself. Unfortunately, when I made a move for it, the sharp end of the pole slipped on the smooth, rounded surface. It flew several feet in front of me. It wasn't exactly how I expected that to play out. A groan escaped my lips as I went to track it down and try again.

I'd only taken a couple of steps when a low chuckle had me turning back.

I looked up to see a guy my age watching me with a giant smile on his face. He wore a Lakers cap and the standard uniform of everyone else out here—a tee-shirt and shorts. His eyes were covered by sunglasses, and in his hand was a metal pole identical to the one I carried.

"Something funny?" I propped the hand that held the trash bag on my hip.

He drew his lips down in a mocking frown and shook his head. "Nope."

"Really? Because I could have sworn I heard you laugh," I snapped, not wanting to deal with this, or any, dude's crap.

"You must be mistaken."

"Whatever," I grumbled, and turned to go after the plastic bottle.

The annoying boy followed me, as I tried to ignore him and focus on my game of hide-and-seek with the soda bottle.

"Word of advice? Don't wear that hat next time."

I stopped. "What?"

His grin was back. "Mrs. Gibbs really hates it when people don't take Helping Hands seriously."

I lifted a single brow. "Oh, yeah? And how do you know that?"

He shrugged. "I've been doing this a long time."

Interesting.

I continued my search. There was a large bush in front of us, and I pushed parts of it this way and that, looking for that stupid bottle. After doing it for longer than reasonable, I abandoned my hunt and began looking for new pieces of trash to put inside my giant bag.

The boy stayed with me.

My feet stopped—again. "Why are you following me?"

He chuckled. "I'm here to keep an eye on you."

"Are you serious?"

"I told you, I've been doing this for a while." He took off his sunglasses, and his eyes showed the same friendliness as his smile. "I'm Jackson, by the way."

"Okay."

He leaned forward and whispered loudly. "This is the part where you tell me your name."

"If you're here to babysit me, shouldn't you already know?"

His laughter rang out, and he shook his head. "Fine, I already know your name is Charlotte. I just wanted to hear it from you."

"Call me Charlie." I pressed my lips together, preventing the smile that wanted to surface.

"All right, Charlie."

He continued to stare at me, and I couldn't stop my own perusal. With his mouth now shut, Jackson was hot— like super, mega hot. His eyes were bright green and friendly, his tan skin was smooth, except for a light stubble on his cheeks, and his dark hair was just long enough that it stuck out in several places from beneath his hat.

It would be incredibly stupid to get involved with a guy the day after my breakup with Anderson, I reminded myself. I needed to keep my head down and avoid trouble for the next eight weeks, not get crushes on guys who got in trouble so much they'd become a regular at Helping Hands.

Of course, that didn't mean I couldn't enjoy how pretty he was to look at.

Afraid I'd been ogling him too long, and unsure of what to say, I started picking up debris with my metal pole again. Jackson followed me, and we picked up trash in uncomfortable silence, sharing the same garbage bag. It was a lot less therapeutic when I wasn't yelling at inanimate objects, and worried about looking like an idiot in front of a cute boy.

"Here," he put his hand out. "Let me carry that."

I looked at him through narrowed eyes. "Why?"

"Because I'm trying to be nice."

I handed the bag over and started stabbing trash again.

"You know, I don't care if you want to keep yelling at the stuff you pick up." I shot him a sharp look, and he raised his hands. "It just looked like you were really into it earlier, and now you're acting like you had a lobotomy."

My eyes widened. Who was this guy?

"Here, I'll even do it with you."

Jackson started jabbing the metal pole into the ground, mumbling and grumbling under his breath. He looked ridiculous.

I let out a quick laugh and shook my head.

"Now, it's your turn."

I stood there debating it for several moments, before nodding. "Fine."

Each time I hit a piece of trash, I said something about Anderson. It felt good to let my anger out, but I soon realized Jackson had stopped and stood to watch me.

"So, what's up with this Anderson guy, anyway? He must have done something pretty bad to earn such hatred from you."

I closed my eyes, not really wanting to go too much into it. "We just broke up yesterday, and I'm still a little bitter about it."

"I'm sorry to hear that."

"He made out with a cheerleader under the bleachers." I lifted one of my shoulders. "I keyed his car."

Jackson laughed. "Seriously?"

"Yeah, it's why I'm out here for the next eight weeks."

"Well, I say let's make sure we really *stick it* to Anderson." He waggled his eyebrows and lifted his pole.

"Oh, no. You're a pun guy?"

He stuck it into the ground, and when he lifted it up, there was another burger wrapper on it. He started beatboxing. "Would you like it better if I was a *wrapper*?"

I groaned. "That's horrible."

Jackson slammed the stick down, and when he brought it up this time, there was a maple leaf on it. "Oh, *leaf* me alone."

"Stop it!" The words were mixed with laughter.

Jackson stopped. "I like to see you smile."

The laughter died on my lips with his comment. "You don't know me well enough to know what you like."

He adjusted his hat and cleared his throat. "Uh, yeah. You're right. I don't know why I said that. Let's just get back to punishing Anderson."

I nodded. "Okay."

We continued walking around our area, just the two of us, picking up trash. We talked a little about recent movies and music, and surprisingly, the time passed quickly.

In fact, the time had been moving so quickly, I didn't realize it was already time for us to be done. Mrs. Gibbs blew a shrill whistle that meant we all needed to gather around.

"This place looks passable. You're free to go. I'll see you next week." I smiled at Jackson, wondering what we would say as we parted ways. Would we exchange numbers? Was I the worst kind of person because I hoped we did even though Anderson and I had just broken up?

But Mrs. Gibbs called him over before we had a chance to speak again. He gave me an apologetic look before walking toward her. I watched him, waiting for him to look back at me, but he never did.

I awkwardly stood there as everyone began to disperse, but Jackson never returned, so I grabbed my bottle and left. Not sure if I was looking forward to seeing him next week or not after that goodbye.

CHAPTER THREE

DARIA LINKED her arm in mine as I walked from the school parking lot up to the main building on Monday morning. Her high, blonde ponytail swayed back and forth with each step we took.

"You never called me this weekend."

"Sorry," I answered lamely.

"And you didn't answer any of my texts."

I shrugged. "My parents limited my internet and texting privileges as extra punishment."

I'd only gotten my wi-fi and data turned back on for my time at Helping Hands after telling my parents I should have it in case I had a hard time finding the group—as if everyone didn't know where Saunders Park was. By the time I got settled into my community service hours, I'd been so distracted by Jackson, I'd forgotten to call or text my best friend.

"And they wouldn't let you send a quick text to let me know you're alive? I was worried about you. I didn't know what happened with Anderson." Her voice became increasingly shrill as she continued. "I had to get my info from Veronica. *Veronica*, of all people. I hate that she knew more about what was going on than I did."

I pulled my arm from Daria's. "Veronica wasn't even there when it happened."

"And yet she still knew more than me. It's my right as your best friend to know what's going on."

I looked at Daria through the corner of my eye. "You mean so you could be the one telling Veronica all about it?"

"Oh, shut up. You know it's not like that."

The thing was, I did know that, but being back on campus after the weekend made me feel angry about the entire situation all over again. And sadly, I was taking it out on Daria.

"Sorry, you're right. But why did you want to know what happened so badly?"

She snorted. "To defend your honor when I saw people posting crap online."

"And are they?"

Daria didn't get a chance to answer because Anderson took that exact moment to peel into the parking lot. The sound of his tires squealing drew our attention to his car, not to mention the attention of the fifteen or so other students walking up to the building. My handiwork was on full display, and a couple of nearby juniors looked over in our direction. They whispered and giggled as they continued to make their way to the school.

"I take that back," Daria said from behind a wide smile. "You don't need any help defending yourself."

I started walking faster, not wanting to come face-to-face with my ex yet. "And that's why I have Saturday work detail."

Daria gasped. "You do?"

Apparently, Veronica hadn't filled her in on that part.

I put my hand on her back and pushed her forward when she tried to slow our pace. "Come on. I'll tell you the rest, but only if we get inside before Anderson has a chance to catch up with us."

She complied, and soon we walked through the front doors of our school and down the hallway filled with students heading to their first class of the day. I recounted Friday's events and quickly learned Veronica knew nothing beyond the video that Linzie took on her phone.

When I mentioned the part about my athletic probation, Daria stopped dead in her tracks. "What?" she screeched, drawing the gazes of everyone near us.

She flipped off the gawkers and pulled me to the side of the hall, right against the lockers that lined it. "But tryouts are coming up."

As if I didn't have October 22nd circled in bright red on my calendar. I'd been counting down the days, almost as eager as Preston to get started. "Yep."

"Well, did Mr. Richards say whether or not you could still be on the team and practice with us?"

I tapped my finger against my lips. "Silly me, I didn't think to ask him while he was threatening to expel me."

"I'm serious, Charlie. This is serious."

"I know it's serious, but there's a lot more I gotta worry about right now besides basketball."

Daria gasped dramatically, but I could see the subtle smile on her lips. "More than basketball? Who are you, and what have you done with my best friend?"

I gave her shoulder a shove, and her expression became somber. "Seriously, Charlie. What are you going to do?"

"I'm not sure yet. I'm facing expulsion." I rubbed my hand over my face. "It won't matter if I get to try out for the team if I don't get to stay at Rosemark."

Daria continued to stare at me. "I can understand you being freaked out. But it sounds like as long as you do your time with Helping Hands, everything should be fine, right?"

I nodded. "Yeah."

"So, it wouldn't hurt to ask Mr. Richards about tryouts." Daria lifted both of her brows and nodded her head encouragingly.

I slowly blinked at my friend.

"We need you as our point guard!"

I shook my head. "You know I'm not the only point guard on the team, right?"

"Yeah, but you're the best."

And I was.

It wasn't arrogance or some kind of puffed up ego. I'd been part of the starting five since my sophomore year. It was why I had basically been named the captain this season before everything happened with Anderson. If we wanted any shot of getting to state this year, I'd need to be on the team.

I let loose a resigned sigh. "I'll see what I can find out after school. But only because I love you."

"Obviously."

Satisfied, Daria started walking again. We pushed through the crowd as we made it to our homeroom class. I got a few dirty looks from the cheerleading squad as we passed by, and I could have sworn I heard someone call me a certain five-letter word.

I wanted to yell and scream at them but remembered the contract—and my probation. I took a deep breath and settled for a saucy wink instead.

"So what are you going to do about Anderson?" Daria asked as we neared our destination.

"What do you mean?"

Daria stuck her hands out in front of her. "Like, are you guys breaking up? Are you getting back together?"

"Are you kidding me?"

"You guys have been dating forever."

I didn't answer right away but instead walked into our class. I went straight to my desk near the back of the room. It was directly in front of Daria's. Once seated, I swiveled to face her. "He kissed Linzie. We are not getting back together."

She lifted her brows.

"I consider what he did with Linzie an intentional foul." I lifted my hands over my head and joined them at the wrist like I was refereeing my life. Someone had to. "I'm not letting him back in the game."

The tardy bell rang, and everyone got in their seats.

Daria still didn't say anything but watched me with a skeptical expression.

"I'm not," I assured her.

"Okay."

"All eyes up here, please," Mrs. Whitmore's voice called from the front of the room.

I gave Daria one last pointed stare. "I'm not."

She nodded, but I swore I heard her whisper, "If you say so," as I turned back around.

APPARENTLY, Daria wasn't the only one who thought Anderson and I were getting back together. Gossip spread through campus faster than Linzie's lips. Between texting, social media, and good old-fashioned word of mouth (aka Veronica O'Rourke), everyone knew what was going on by lunchtime. I heard the whispers and, since my mom conceded I needed my phone at school, even snuck a glance at Snapchat between classes. I knew there were several different versions of the story going around, and very few of them were accurate. Or, at least, I hoped they weren't.

I felt like I was going to be sick when I walked into the

cafeteria that afternoon, but I did it because I had to. Everyone would be watching and waiting to see what happened next in the Anderson and Charlie show. I had no desire to star in another low-budget high school documentary—after the first one landed me with Saturday work detail and athletic probation—but, I also refused to back down. If I hid out in the library, the rumors would only get worse.

So, I walked in, head held high, with Daria beside me. We grabbed our lunches from the line and made our way to our seat. In no time, Pres and his girlfriend, Beth, sat down next to Daria and me, blue plastic trays in hand. My brother sat down in the seat normally reserved for Anderson making a loud statement to everyone without saying a word.

Anderson wasn't welcome at our table anymore.

He shoved a massive bite of shepherd's pie into his mouth. "Anderson talked to me yesterday," he said around the mouthful like it wasn't a big deal.

I looked up from where I was moving mashed potatoes around on my plate. I remembered Preston leaving the house on Sunday afternoon, but he hadn't said anything about Anderson, so I figured it was just another Taco Bell run. "What did he say?"

Preston shrugged. "He wanted to know whose side I was on."

I sat up. "And what did you say?"

Preston pressed his lips together as he fought a smile.

Beth smacked him in the arm. "He acted like an idiot. What is it about guys and throwing punches?"

My eyes widened. "You didn't!"

He pointed to where Anderson sat. When I looked over, my ex-boyfriend was watching me with unrestrained malice in his eyes. Even from here, I could see his bottom lip was swollen and had a large gash in it.

I turned back to Preston. "You shouldn't have done that," I cried. "Mr. Richards is going to put you on athletic probation too."

He shook his head. "Nah, don't worry, Brooks isn't getting off that easy."

"Of course, you'd make this about you and your stupid rivalry, but I don't want to see you get in trouble."

"Don't worry. Anderson isn't going to say anything, and I'm not going to get in trouble."

"But—"

"First of all," he interrupted. "Everyone knows it's my duty as your brother to protect your honor." I rolled my eyes. What was it about everyone and my honor? "And second of all, if Anderson went and tattled like some little baby and made it so one of the starting five couldn't actually, you know, start, there'd be quite a few angry teammates to deal with."

"Okay." I sighed. "But I still don't like the idea of you punching someone, Pres. Violence never solved anything."

My brother chuckled. "Says the girl who vandalized his car."

"Says the girl with Saturday work detail." My voice

was little more than a mumble. I grabbed the roll from my plate and took a bite. "I've learned my lesson. I'm going to be completely straitlaced from here on out."

Unfortunately, the erupting laughter from everyone at the table wasn't exactly encouraging.

CHAPTER FOUR

MY PHONE BUZZED LOUDLY on my nightstand.

Was it seriously Saturday morning again? Already?

I grabbed it to turn off the 7:30 alarm, only to see my screen lit up with a bunch of texts from Anderson that were sent in the middle of the night. It was way too freaking early to deal with this.

3:46 AM
Anderson: We should talk.
Anderson: I'm sorry.
Anderson: I miss you.
Anderson: Linzie doesn't mean anything.
Anderson: Are we still going to Homecoming together?

The time stamp was from just a couple of hours ago,

and I couldn't help but wonder if he was up late drinking and partying. His desire to take everything too far was one of the things that had bugged me about Anderson when we were dating. Now that we were officially over, I hated it.

I sent a string of texts his way and crossed my fingers that he was hungover.

7:33 *AM*
Charlie: We
Charlie: Are
Charlie: Not
Charlie: Dating
Charlie: And there is no way I'm going to Homecoming with you!!! Don't text me again. Do you understand???

I could only hope that made it clear enough for him.

I'd spent the week grateful he was ignoring me, and that we somehow had avoided a huge blowout. By Wednesday, people had given up hope for anything beyond his graffitied car door, and I'd focused on being the best-behaved student on probation I could be. Sure, I was still pretty pissed, but I had priorities.

I needed to stay at Rosemark High, and I needed to play on the varsity team.

I quickly got dressed in similar clothing as the week before, choosing a simple Nike hat instead of my sarcastic one. Hopefully, Mrs. Gibbs wouldn't put me in BFE that way. I did give myself more than a passing look in the mirror, however. I wasn't sure if Jackson would be there again, but wanted to look okay, just in case.

I quickly left my room, walked past Preston's closed door and out to the kitchen. Like the previous Saturday, my mom was sitting at the kitchen table. Only this time, there was a homemade egg and cheese sandwich on a plate in front of her.

"I knew you'd be racing out of here again and wanted to make sure you had something hearty this morning."

This woman might not have given birth to me, but she loved me as if I were her own daughter. And she was truly Mom to me—not Carol, or Mrs. Royce. I couldn't imagine my life without her, and the fact that she kept waking up early on Saturday to make sure I was well fed warmed my heart.

I grabbed the still-warm sandwich from the plate and took a bite. "This is perfect," I said while still chewing. "Thanks, Mom."

She smiled up at me. "Be good."

"I make no promises," I teased before I leaned in and kissed her cheek. I grabbed my keys from the hook and left for another fun-filled day with Marlowe Junction's Helping Hands.

WHEN I PULLED up to Saunders Park, I was surprised to see most of the kids were different from the previous

Saturday. There were a couple of new people I recognized from Rosemark and several completely unfamiliar faces. Whether they were from Pinebrook, or even the private school on the edge of town, St. Joseph's, I couldn't be sure.

Like last time, Mrs. Gibbs wasted no time barking orders to everyone. She looked me up and down as I put on my best sugary-sweet smile. With a grunt of approval, she sent me to paint picnic tables alone under a pavilion. I sent a quick thanks heavenward and grabbed a bucket of white paint and a brush.

I listened as quite a few people went to the "north quadrant" and wondered if that was where all new recruits were sent. Maybe my assignment had nothing to do with the hat I wore last time. Not that it mattered. I'd had a good time after all.

I got started, ignoring the small pang that formed in my stomach. It was ridiculous to think I'd get to work with Jackson again this week, and more than a little embarrassing that I wanted to so badly.

I pulled my earbuds from my pocket and cranked my music up.

It took me a couple of minutes, and three broken stir sticks, before I finally got the can of paint open. But once I got past that, it was smooth sailing. I started with the table part of the bench so I could sit down while I worked. Once I did the seats, it would be standing room only under the pavilion.

I danced in my seat and hummed under my breath as I

finished the first coat. When I stood up to admire my work and move on to the next section, I bumped into something. Or, more accurately, someone.

"Ahhh!" I yelled, startled to realize I wasn't alone. I ripped out my earbuds and was met with the pleasant and familiar sound of Jackson laughing.

I smacked his arm. "You scared me!" I hit him again. "You can't just walk up on people like that."

He lifted his hands in surrender, and I noticed that he had a paintbrush in one of them. "Sorry." A corner of his mouth lifted in a smile.

"Wait," I said slowly. "How long have you been standing there?"

He looked down at his feet, but I could see the stupid smile still stuck to his face.

"Oh, my goodness!" My cheeks warmed, and I was sure they were bright red. "Please tell me you didn't see me singing and dancing."

"Would it help if I said it was super adorable?"

I closed my eyes and shook my head. "No, it most definitely wouldn't."

"What if I said you were off-tune and have no rhythm?"

My eyes snapped open, and I was met with his smiling face once more. His green eyes twinkled with humor and any embarrassment I'd felt melted away. It had only been a week, but I'd already forgotten how cute Jackson was.

Darn him.

Today, he was sans hat, so his brown hair was on full display. It stuck out in a couple different places, and I wondered if he rolled out of bed and came straight to the park. He wore a Lakers tee and gym shorts.

I smiled at him and tipped my head toward the paintbrush. "Does that mean I'm saddled with you again today?"

His hand went to his chest. "Ouch, Charlie. I'm crushed."

I snorted. "Oh, yeah. I'm sure you're really broken up inside."

He laughed and lifted his paintbrush. "Actually, I'm here to help."

I eyed him suspiciously. "Help? Or keep an eye on me again?"

"Can it be a little bit of both?"

"I guess. As long as you come over here and actually pull your weight."

He playfully shook his head as he came over. And, in no time, we were painting the seat I'd just occupied.

"So, what gives with all the new faces today?" I asked as I dipped my brush into the paint can once again.

"What do you mean?"

"Um, that there are a ton of different people than last week. I don't recognize anyone except for you."

Jackson shrugged. "Yeah, most people are only here for a week or two."

A week or two? And here, I'd been sentenced for two months of this crap!

"Really?" I asked, somewhat disbelieving.

He nodded, though his gaze was still focused on the task at hand. "I was actually surprised to see you again this week. I figured you would be done after last Saturday."

"Is that why you disappeared so quickly?"

I grimaced at how accusatory I sounded. Not that I had any right to be upset that he didn't hang out and talk to me after we'd finished picking up trash.

"Yeah, sorry about that. My..." he cleared his throat. "Um, Mrs. Gibbs needed to talk to me about something."

"Did you give her the full report on me?"

"Something like that," he smiled at me. "It took a little longer than I thought, and when I went back, you were gone."

"Well, don't worry. I've got six more weeks after today."

"Then, I look forward to seeing you for six more weeks."

Wow. What had this guy done?

He'd admitted he'd been doing this for a while, and he thought he'd still be here at least as long as me? That alone should have made me cautious, but for some reason, I felt safe around him.

"So, what's up with all the Lakers stuff?" I asked. When he looked at me in question, I clarified. "Well, last week you wore a Lakers hat, today it's a shirt. What gives?"

"Why are you paying so much attention to what I'm wearing? Have you been checking me out? I'm more than some piece of meat for your viewing pleasure, you know."

"You are such a dork."

He laughed. "I don't know. I'm a big LeBron fan."

"Ugh." I rolled my eyes. "Of course, you would pick him. People who don't know anything about basketball always pick LeBron as their favorite player." I leaned in and stage-whispered: "He's my mom's favorite too."

"With good reason."

"Yeah, because he's overrated."

"Over—?" Jackson made a strangled sound and put a fist to his mouth. "Overrated? People know who he is because he's the best player in the NBA right now. That's why he's everyone's favorite."

"Oh, please. Chris Paul is so much better."

He raised his brows.

"What? It's not his fault he was saddled with Blake Griffin for so long."

Jackson tipped his head in acknowledgment. "Yeah, I'll give you that, but LeBron is more than just a great player." He started listing reasons he was a fanboy on his fingers. "He speaks out against racial inequality, he opened a school in his hometown, he sends kids to college. Plus, he's been with his wife forever."

All good reasons.

I let out a long sigh. "Fine, you're allowed to like LeBron, but Chris Paul is still my favorite."

Jackson smiled. "I'm impressed you know so much about basketball."

"Seriously?" I stopped painting and narrowed my eyes at him. "I didn't take you for that guy."

"What guy is that?"

"The kind who doesn't think girls can like basketball. Or, am I supposed to act like I'm an idiot?" I pouted my lips and lifted my finger to them. "Remind me, basketball has three innings?"

"Yeah, please don't ever say that again," Jackson said with a grimace.

"Then don't patronize me."

He nodded. "You've got yourself a deal."

"Good, because saying that felt way too wrong."

We started painting again but, this time, I had to fight hard to keep the corners of my mouth from lifting into a goofy smile. Like the week before, our conversation quickly moved through one subject to another. And as Jackson and I worked, we found a comfortable rhythm.

We were just finishing the last section when I jokingly called him a goody-two-shoes.

"What are you talking about?" he asked.

I shrugged. "I'm just saying, you can't be all that bad if Mrs. Gibbs is sending you to watch over the other troublemakers."

"Oh, I'm totally bad."

"Sure, you are." I laughed.

"I can prove it." He leaned in closer, and I found myself completely distracted by the scent of his cologne. Too distracted to see the dangerous glint in his eye, and too distracted to see his right hand reaching up, or the paintbrush in it. Jackson tapped it gently against my nose.

It was wet. I lifted my hand to my face, and when I

pulled my fingers away, I saw white on their tips. My mouth fell open.

"Told you so." He jumped up and started running away.

"Oh, you're a dead man!"

I chased him with my paintbrush with every intention of getting him back. He weaved in and out of people who were on trash duty today. They watched him with confusion and then turned those same expressions to me when they realized I was in hot pursuit.

When I caught up to Jackson, I fully intended to wipe paint all over his stupid face. He laughed as he stayed just out of reach. Every time I got close, he would use his long arms to keep me away. No matter how much I squirmed and tried to fake him out, I couldn't get close enough to get him back.

So, I did the only thing I could think of.

I fell to my knees, careful to keep my paintbrush from touching the dirt. "Ow!" I cried loud enough to draw everyone's attention.

Jackson stopped. "Are you okay?" he asked, his voice cautious as he kept a safe distance.

"Yeah, I think so." I stood up but whimpered as I set my left foot to the ground. "I think I tripped over a root." I started limping toward the pavilion, forcing my face to stay turned away from Jackson. If he saw the grin on it, my cover would be blown.

I continued to make my way to the picnic table,

intently listening as his footsteps got closer. And closer. And closer.

I felt his presence beside me before he spoke. "Charlie, are you—"

Splat!

Jackson's eyes widened as the paintbrush connected with his cheek. A big blob of white spread from his ear to his lips, just narrowly missing his mouth. I dropped the paintbrush, and ran, but not fast enough.

Soon strong arms were circling around my waist, and lifting me from the ground. His cologne hit my nostrils again, and I fought the urge to close my eyes and inhale deeply. Instead, I wriggled to break free. His responding laughter rumbled deep in his chest, and I could feel it against my back as he continued to hold tight.

"Let me go!" I yelled, drawing more attention our way, but I didn't care.

"Not until you admit I'm not a goodie-two-shoes."

I shook my shoulders back and forth. "Jackson."

"Fine." He released me, and I sprinted a few paces away. I bounced on the balls of my feet, ready to run if he started coming at me.

He wiped the paint from his face and rubbed it on his shorts. "You don't play fair."

I smiled wide. "I never claimed to."

Mrs. Gibbs came over, a stern look on her face. "Glad to see you're having fun over here. Charlie, clean this mess up. You"—she looked at Jackson—"come with me."

I watched as Mrs. Gibbs and Jackson walked away. I could only imagine what she was telling the boy who was supposed to be keeping an eye on me. Still, I didn't regret it.

As she led Jackson towards the parking lot, Mrs. Gibbs stopped and talked to a girl my age who had been busy pulling weeds. The director pointed in my direction, and the girl started walking over. She was petite in every way— less than five feet tall with short blonde hair.

"Mrs. Gibbs told me to come over and help you with the mess you made."

"Okay, thanks," I said still watching Jackson. I really hoped our flirting didn't tack more weeks on to his never-ending string of Saturdays with Helping Hands.

The girl followed my gaze and turned back to me. "Might as well give up that dream now."

I turned to face her, irritated I was so transparent. Of course, I'd just chased him around the park giggling like a schoolgirl, so what did I expect? "What do you mean?"

She sighed and pointed to where Mrs. Gibbs and Jackson stood talking. "Brooks. All the girls at Pinebrook are in love with him. He's a shameless flirt, but he never dates."

"Wait. I thought his name was Jackson?" I asked dumbly as my mind struggled to make connections it didn't want to.

"Yeah," the girl said slowly. "But everyone calls him Brooks. It's his last name."

Brooks.

Pinebrook?

Jackson Brooks was more than a cute boy who liked the Lakers. He also played for Pinebrook and was one of the best forwards in Marlowe Junction.

Not to mention, he was my brother's biggest enemy.

Oh, crap.

CHAPTER FIVE

DARIA GRABBED me in the hall on Monday morning wearing a silk robe tied around her waist and a sleeping mask over her hair like a headband. She had colorful socks on her feet that were barely covered by the slippers she wore as shoes.

She looked like a perfect picture of someone getting ready for bed.

"I seriously hate spirit week," I said, allowing my friend to link her arm in mine.

"You say that every year."

"And I mean it every year," I argued. "It's dumb that the football team gets five days of dressing up."

"It's meant to get that Mountaineer team spirit going." Daria smiled at a girl who wore a similar get-up who walked in the opposite direction. They even went so far as to give each other a high five as they passed by. "See? I never talk to her, but we get to share in that one special moment because of school pride."

"And wearing your pajamas to school is supposed to garner that camaraderie?" I asked. "Or any of the other themed days? Like, what does dressing like a tourist have to do with the Mountaineers? Or your favorite sports player? Honestly, dressing up like someone from another team seems like it would detract from school spirit."

"Whatever." She rolled her eyes. "You like dressing up. You're just being stubborn."

"You're right, I do. But I wear my normal clothing purely on principle. I'll start dressing up when they dedicate a week to Rosemark's basketball teams."

Daria snorted. "Which means you won't be dressing up anytime soon." She paused. "Unless you're going to Sammi's Halloween party?"

Daria had been hounding me about it ever since the captain of the cheerleading squad invited everyone to come to her house while her parents were out of town. It was just dumb luck it fell so close to Halloween.

"Do you think I really want to go to her party? Cheerleaders are bad enough on their own. I definitely don't want to go to Linzie's best friend's house." I didn't like the way she watched me in the halls ever since I caught her making out with my boyfriend. Linzie acted like I was the bad guy here, which was completely insane. She was the one who made out with my boyfriend!

"Oh, come on. You know Sammi's parties are more than just the preppy kids. Everyone will be there, including the boys from St. Joseph's." She waggled her eyes.

"Stop being so boy crazy!" I playfully pushed Daria away from me.

She shrugged as she laughed it off because we both knew she was anything but. Daria hadn't dated anyone as long as I had known her, always claiming she wasn't interested in any of the guys in Marlowe Junction.

And I'd definitely had my fill of guys in our small town. Between my ex, my brother, and my teeny, tiny infatuation with his enemy, I was good for a lifetime.

"Just think about it, Charlie. It's our senior year. We should be taking advantage of every possible chance to live out our high school days."

"That sounds like something straight from a motivational poster."

"And you sound like a boring, old lady with twenty cats who's too afraid to leave the house. Stop being so lame."

I stopped and fixed her with a look. "Either I be the lame old lady who stays on the straight and narrow, or I kiss basketball and college scholarships goodbye. I can't risk it."

She rolled her eyes. "Mr. Richards can't fault you for dressing up and going to a party, Charlie. You're taking this community service, probation thing too far. Live a little."

A corner of my mouth lifted. "Maybe."

"Definitely," she argued.

"I'll think about it."

"Think about what?" a male voice said from beside me. I looked over and saw Anderson standing far too close for comfort. I'd been so absorbed with my argument with Daria, I hadn't even noticed his approach.

Anderson was dressed up for pajama day in a thick terry robe draped over a tee shirt and basketball shorts. On his feet were white socks and slip-on sandals. He slung his arm over my shoulder as he stopped at my side.

My gaze quickly found some of the guys standing a safe distance away. I saw Jeremiah, Mackey, and a few others from the team, but no Preston. The guys struggled to make eye contact with me as I looked at them. Jeremiah shifted from foot to foot.

Whatever was about to go down wasn't going to be good.

I twisted out of his grip and gave him an irritated look. "What do you want, Anderson?"

"Can't a guy say hi to his girlfriend in the hall?" His smile caused a shudder to go through me.

It was weird how knowing one thing about someone could change how you interpreted everything that came from them. Anderson's smile, for example. There was a time when he could lift those lips, and the butterflies in my stomach would come to life. Now, as I imagined the way he kissed another with them, his smile only made me feel icky—and anxious.

I held my breath as I waited for him to strike.

"Actually, I was just talking to the guys about your lack of costume."

I cocked my head. "What?"

"You know, why you're not wearing anything special for pajama day."

I'd literally just been having this conversation with Daria. Had he been listening in? "Uh, because I don't want to participate in spirit week?"

The sound of Anderson chuckling raised the hairs on the back of my neck. "It's okay. You don't have to be shy. I already told the guys the reason you don't have pajamas is—"

"I have pajamas."

"—because you sleep naked." The words were loud enough to gain the attention of several people in the hall.

"You don't know what I sleep in," I grated, but the damage had already been done.

I looked around, and people were already whispering and raising their eyebrows. They'd heard just enough to form their own conclusions, and it would be everywhere by the end of the day.

Anderson and Charlie were sleeping together.

Yeah, right!

I was half tempted to call up Veronica, Rosemark's very own gossip girl, just to make sure the truth was what circulated. I wanted to scream at Anderson, yell at everyone who stood watching out of the corners of their eyes, call my brother up and ask him where the heck he was.

But I didn't do any of those things.

I stormed away down the hall, not bothering to walk in

the direction of my class. Mrs. Whitmore would just have to survive without me. Daria chased close behind. When I walked out the double doors and started moving toward the parking lot, she grabbed my arm.

"What are you doing?"

I shook my head frantically. "I gotta get out of here."

"But school hasn't even started." Her face was etched with concern.

"Yeah, and Anderson is already being a jerk. I can't be around him. Not today."

Not after the wonderful and awful Saturday I had with Jackson Brooks, I thought to myself, unwilling to share those details with anyone—not even Daria.

I continued to stomp toward the parking lot determined to escape for a few minutes in the safety of the car my brother and I shared. When I looked at the spot Preston parked in that morning, I stopped dead in my tracks.

The car was gone.

I turned to Daria. "Where is my car?"

She lifted her hands. "Don't look at me."

"Crap!" I shouted. "Crap, crap, crap!"

I stood there silently, staring at the empty spot. But no amount of time would make the missing vehicle appear. That was unless Preston decided to pull back in—which he didn't.

"Crap," I said one last time for good measure, not wanting to go back to school.

The tardy bell rang in the distance, and Daria watched me, her feet facing the school, her body turned to go inside.

I waved at her. "Go ahead. I'll be right there."

She continued to stare at me.

"Seriously. I'm fine. I'll just be a couple of minutes late."

Daria stood there for a moment longer, before finally turning her body completely and walking toward the front of the building.

Once I was alone, I let out a frustrated growl. This really sucked. I didn't want to deal with Anderson. Any other time, I might have been able to face him with an equally conniving attitude. But not right now, not with so much on the line.

I sat down on the curb and pulled my phone out. There were no missed messages, so I scrolled aimlessly, not really reading what was on the screen. I just needed something to do while I waited for my annoyance to recede enough to go to class. When I was sure I could return without feeling like I was going to explode, I stood up, wiped the dirt from the back of my pants, and walked toward the building.

Unfortunately, once I made it through the front door, I saw my principal standing just on the other side—almost like he was waiting for me.

"Miss Royce."

I gave him a tight smile. "Mr. Richards."

"Why don't you come with me to my office?"

I followed him silently, mentally cursing myself for

getting in trouble once again. I'd just needed a few minutes to escape, so I didn't do something idiotic, and now I worried I'd sabotaged myself anyway.

We entered into his office, and I sat down in my all-too-familiar seat across from him.

"I caught your friend, Daria, walking in late. Since Miss Williams never breaks the rules, I gave her a free pass. Imagine my surprise when I walked her to homeroom, and you were missing."

"I couldn't have just been, you know, absent?" The words were out before I could stop them, and I knew I was digging my hole even deeper.

"Believe it or not, Miss Royce, I am not the bad guy. And I am not out to get you. The rules we have at Rosemark are for you and your fellow students' protection."

I exhaled. "And I get that. I do. But I needed a minute to collect myself."

Mr. Richards sat quietly and leaned back in his chair as he waited for the rest of my explanation. When it dawned on him that it wasn't coming, he sighed and sat back up. "Miss Royce, you are already committed to several weeks with Marlowe Junction's Helping Hands, in addition to athletic probation. I'm not sure what else to do here to make you understand the serious nature of your behavior."

I stared at my feet.

"I don't want to expel you, Charlie." I looked up, my eyes wide. He chuckled. "I don't, but you have to understand that many of the underclassmen look up to you."

I shook my head. "No, they don't."

Everyone knew the football players and cheerleaders were the top of the high school hierarchy. Next were the boys' baseball and basketball teams. Girls' basketball was just above girls' softball and soccer. Then, of course, theater, band, and art were also somewhere in the mix.

Regardless, I wasn't anyone's role model, and that was perfectly fine with me.

"They do," Mr. Richards argued. "And they see your behavior as an example. They want to be cool like Charlie Royce. I already have a clique of freshmen girls who were caught cutting the ponytails of some of the dance team. When I asked them why they did it, they said it was because of you."

"But that was before they were even in high school," I argued.

"You don't think the stories of your notoriety get handed down to each new class?"

Uh, no. I didn't.

"The point is I have to make an example of you."

"Wait. That's what all of this is about? My life is on the line because you want to scare a bunch of fourteen-year-olds?"

I barely contained the anger that simmered beneath the surface. I wanted to report him to the school board, to yell and scream, but there was also a part of me that acknowledged my principal's right to punish me after years of acting out.

"It's not the only reason, no. But it's part of it. I have a responsibility to this school."

So my punishment was just part of a bigger picture? The thought didn't exactly make me feel all warm and fuzzy inside.

I knew it wasn't a good time to ask, but I had to know. I was sick of all this fear of discipline and not knowing if I could play. I was going to stop stressing myself out over every little thing I did on campus.

Plus, I knew Daria would be dying to know.

"Speaking of my punishments." I took a deep breath. "I was wondering, can I still try out for the basketball team while on athletic probation? My eight weeks with Helping Hands will be up around the start of the season."

Mr. Richards tipped his chin, allowing the abrupt change in our topic of conversation. "You are welcome to go to tryouts. Just make sure it's abundantly clear to your coach that you can't play until your probation is finished."

My shoulders tensed. The idea of telling Coach that her starting point guard would be out of commission at the season-opening was almost as scary as the expulsion I still faced, but I nodded.

"And, Miss Royce." I looked up. "I'm not going to give you detention for being late today, but I need you to understand something. This is your last get-out-of-jail-free card. The next time I catch you ditching school, or acting anything less than the ideal student, we're going to have to have a serious meeting to revisit your contract. Do you understand?"

"Yes, Mr. Richards."

"Good." He signed a small yellow slip of paper

excusing my tardiness and handed it to me. "Now, go to class."

I left his office and went directly to Mrs. Whitmore's class. I did not pass Go, I did not collect $200.

I handed her the slip and walked toward my desk in the back, careful to keep my head down and not make eye contact with anyone. I swore I heard snickering from Sammi and Linzie's direction, but I didn't look at them. I quietly slid into my seat and kept my head facing forward.

I felt a tap on my shoulder. "Psst. What happened?"

I gave a small shake of my head.

"Are you okay?"

I gave a quick nod.

"Charlie?"

I let out an impatient breath and quickly scribbled "I'll talk to you later," on a piece of paper and handed it back to her, careful to avoid getting caught by our teacher.

"I've heard that before," Daria muttered under her breath. I wanted to tell her I meant it this time but didn't risk another word.

CHAPTER SIX

PRESTON'S and my car magically reappeared after school, although I hadn't seen my brother roaming the halls or at lunch that day. He stood next to our vehicle as I walked out, looking down at his phone.

When I got close, he looked up and smiled at me. "What took you so long?"

Silently, I got into the passenger seat. I slammed the door shut and waited. Soon, the driver's side door was opening, and Pres was sliding into his place next to me.

"Charlie, what's wrong?" he asked. His brows were lowered as he turned to face me head-on.

"Where were you today?" I snapped, not bothering to hide my irritation.

Preston's gaze faltered. "Um, what do you mean?"

I pressed my lips together and let out a long breath through my nose. "I mean, I came out to the car earlier, and it was gone. And then you were suspiciously missing from lunch and the halls all day. Not to mention, I always beat you to the car because you always spend, like, ten minutes making out with Beth after school."

His eyes widened.

"Oh, like it's a secret. I'm not an idiot, Pres." I lifted my hands. "Where were you?"

My brother ran a hand over his face. "I was practicing."

"Practicing what?" My voice was incredulous.

After a brief pause, he answered under his breath. "Basketball." His cheeks turned a deep shade of red that matched his hair. "Tryouts are next week, and I want to make sure I'm ready."

"Ready?" I rolled my eyes. "Ready for what, Pres? It's a high school team, not the NBA. You don't need to skip school to sharpen your skills, especially when you already know you're gonna make varsity *and* the starting five."

My brother shifted in the driver's seat, still unable to look at me. There was more to the story, and I could see the moment his resolve broke.

"Fine," he said. "It's this competition with Brooks. I heard that he spent the summer going all over the country doing different basketball training camps."

"Really?" I asked, barely stopping myself from telling him how I thought Brooks had probably spent the summer volunteering for Helping Hands. "Who'd you hear that from?"

"Beth said she overheard Veronica talking about it in the bathroom last week."

I pressed my fingers to my temples. "So you're telling me you skipped school to train for a high school basketball team based on a rumor your girlfriend heard in the bathroom?"

"When you put it that way..." Preston looked down at the center console of the car. "Please don't tell Mom and Dad."

"I'm not going to tattle on you, Pres," I assured him. "But I'm guessing the guys on the team all knew?"

He nodded, a crease forming between his eyes.

"I guess that explains why Anderson was talking crap to me this morning."

Preston's head snapped up. "What are you talking about?"

I told him what happened, but added, "And don't you dare attack Anderson again," when I was finished. "I know you said that punching him made you guys even in some weird macho way, but I have a feeling that if you go after him again, he's gonna keep harassing me. I just want this thing with him to be over. Okay?"

"But—"

"Okay?" I repeated, my voice firm.

He didn't answer right away.

"I'd really hate for our parents to find out you skipped school today."

And I really hated that I was blackmailing him. The irritation in his eyes was clear, but desperate times called for desperate measures. I didn't want my brother making things worse when I was already struggling to get my life back to normal.

He eventually nodded. "Okay. But I should have been there today, and I owe you one now."

After giving me one last look of concern, Preston put the car in drive. We didn't talk a lot on the trip, both lost in our thoughts from the day.

Still grumpy at Preston for skipping school, I could barely concentrate on my homework once we were at our house. After an hour of what I considered more than a valiant effort, I gave up and looked at my phone for a welcome distraction. A text from an unknown number filled my home screen. It had been sent half an hour earlier, but I'd somehow missed the telltale buzz.

3:02 *PM*
Hey, this is Jackson. Is this Charlie?

Jackson was texting me? I glanced around as if my brother could see through the walls. Once I was satisfied he couldn't, I wasn't sure if I wanted to smile or throw my phone against the wall. Not to mention, how the heck had Jackson gotten my phone number? I messaged him back.

Charlie: Wait. Is this Jackson... or BROOKS? And how did you get my number?

I hit send and waited.

And waited.

When Jackson or Brooks or whatever I was supposed to call him didn't text me back after a stomach-churning five minutes, I put my phone down and went outside to shoot some hoops. I threw shot after shot and quickly realized this is what I should have done as soon as we got home.

It was incredibly therapeutic to throw the ball at our crappy little hoop in our driveway. The way my muscles burned as I pushed myself harder and harder made me feel alive. I didn't know how long I spent outside, but I'd almost forgotten my terrible day at school, Preston's absence, and the weird text Jackson sent me by the time my parents called me in for dinner.

"How was your day?" Dad asked as the four of us sat around the dinner table.

"Fine," Pres and I answered in unison.

Our dad's brows creased as he looked back and forth between the two of us and our overly cheerful smiles.

Oh, yeah. We were great at this.

"Did something happen?"

"No." The word came from both of us once again. For not being twins—or even siblings by blood—we sure had a creepy *The Shining* vibe going on. I kicked my brother under the table as he shot me a look that said, "shut up."

"What's going on?" Mom asked. "And don't even think about saying nothing. We weren't born yesterday."

Preston opened his mouth, but I beat him to it.

"Anderson was being a jerk today." The words spilled out quickly.

"Oh, honey." Her voice was soft.

"And I asked Preston not to say anything because I was embarrassed because I... I still like him." It was a lie, and the words tasted vile on my tongue. I hoped Preston appreciated the way I was covering for him.

"Charlie-bear," my dad said. "You don't have to be embarrassed. Feelings are complicated, and we can't always control them."

I nodded my head with the appropriate amount of thoughtful consideration.

"But I hope you realize a guy who cheats on you and then says unkind things to you is not the kind of guy you want to date." He gave a quick glance to Mom, and I felt like the worst kind of jerk. I hadn't even considered her ex-husband, Preston's biological father.

Preston and I were never given the full scoop of what happened in her first marriage, but we both knew it wasn't good. All of our knowledge was based on some of Preston's foggy memories and the type of relationship lectures we were given once we both were allowed to date.

Dad continued. "As much as we were disappointed to hear you keyed Anderson's car, he is not the kind of guy we want you dating. I'm glad you aren't together anymore."

I continued to nod my head.

"And, Preston?" He turned to my brother who was looking down at the plate in front of him, and I hoped he wasn't thinking too hard on his jerk of a sperm-donor father.

"Yeah?"

"I know you can't be everywhere at once, and you can't prevent these things from happening, but I want you to promise me you'll look after Charlie. Can you do that, Son?"

"Yeah," Preston answered, his gaze still trained on the food in front of him.

The rest of the meal was more than just a little uncomfortable. My dad tried over and over again to draw conversation from the three of us, but it just wasn't happening. There were too many painful memories swirling around the table.

From Preston and Mom's past with her ex-husband to my relationship with Anderson, none of us felt cheery enough to talk over dinner. When my brother and I were excused from the table, we both practically jumped out of our seats to rush out of the kitchen.

Preston lingered at the door to his room. "Thanks for covering for me in there," he said quietly.

I nodded. "Sorry if I brought up bad memories."

He shrugged. "It's okay. I think your dad is really great for my mom. I'm sure he'll have her laughing before bedtime."

I gave him a tight smile. "I hope so."

We stood in awkward silence.

Preston hitched his thumb at his door. "I think I'm just

gonna hide out in my room for the rest of the night. Good-night, Charlie."

"Night, Pres."

I walked down the short distance to my room and shut the door. Once I was sitting down on my bed, I checked my phone for missed calls or texts.

I hadn't saved Jackson as a contact in my phone, unsure what to put him under. The possibilities were endless. There was Jackson, Brooks, brother's biggest enemy, arch-nemesis, etc. But I knew the text from an unknown number that lit up my screen was from him.

5:53 PM

Jackson: Please don't be mad.

Charlie: Did you know Preston was my brother?

Jackson: I wondered when I saw your last name on the Helping Hands' roster.

Charlie: Is that how you got my number? Stealing the roster?? Are you trying to use me to get to him?

Jackson: What? No! I've had a really fun time with you these last two weeks, and I stole your number from my aunt because I wanted to see if you wanted to hang out sometime outside of Helping Hands.

Charlie: Your aunt?

Jackson: Lol. Mrs. Gibbs. It's why I'm there every week. (Looks good on college applications.)

Charlie: Not because you're a troublemaker?

Jackson: Sorry to disappoint you.

I couldn't stop the puff of air—that was dangerously close to a laugh—from escaping my lips.

Charlie: And you don't mind spending time with one?

Wait. Crap. Now, I was flirting with him.

Jackson: Are you saying you want to hang out sometime?
Charlie: I'm saying I'll think about it. I don't like people lying to me.
Jackson: I know you think I did it on purpose, but I swear it wasn't like that. I told you my name was Jackson because I didn't want to be "Brooks" around you. There's a reputation that comes with that name.

I thought about what the girl at Helping Hands had said to me as another text popped up on the screen.

Jackson: I swear I didn't realize you were Royce's sister until I looked at the volunteer list tonight. And even then, I wasn't sure. You don't look anything like him.

His argument made sense. Part of me wanted to say yes to spending time with him, but there was another part of my brain telling me this was a bad idea. Preston would never approve.

I didn't know what to say, so I chickened out and pulled the sleepy card.

Charlie: I gotta go to bed. Why don't you try again tomorrow?

I added a single winking emoji for good measure and held my breath, anxious to see how he'd respond. Thankfully, he didn't keep me waiting. His answering text came quickly.

Jackson: Parting is such sweet sorrow that I shall say goodnight till it be morrow.

I recognized those words, but it took me a minute to figure out why. They were from a play we'd studied a couple of years ago.

For being a star athlete, it looked like Jackson was a bit of a dork. I wasn't sure that was a bad thing. The smile returned unbidden to my lips.

Charlie: Just so you know, I'm not drinking poison for you.
Jackson: Just so you know, Juliet used a dagger.

I laughed out loud this time.

Charlie: Yeah, I'm not doing that either, Romeo.
Jackson: Fiiiine. Talk to you tomorrow, Juliet.

I waited to see if Jackson would send anything else.

When he didn't, I was disappointed even though I'd told him I was going to bed. At least I now knew what to save him as in my phone. I typed "Romeo" into my contacts, put my phone on its charger, and fell asleep with the sneaking suspicion a certain brown-haired boy would be invading my dreams.

CHAPTER SEVEN

THE REST of the week was...difficult, to say the least.

Preston got weirdly protective, Anderson kept giving me dirty looks every chance he got, and Daria wouldn't stop talking about basketball tryouts. The combination of all of that made me feel like I was going crazy!

One of the only things making me feel normal was texting with Jackson. It wasn't all that often—just little things about our day or memes we liked—but it was fun.

I liked Jackson.

I just hated that I had to keep him a secret from everyone. Not only was he enemy number one to Preston—which he was—but school pride was a big deal in Marlowe Junction. The rivalry between Rosemark and Pinebrook was universal across all sports, but especially basketball.

I should have been avoiding him on pure principle.

So when my alarm went off on Saturday morning, I

was nervous, to say the least. I was excited to see him but still wasn't sure how I was supposed to act around him.

I quickly put on a dress shirt and khakis, since we were going to the nursing home that morning instead of Saunders Park, and walked down the hallway to eat a quick breakfast. I'd promised my mom I would eat something substantial this time, which meant waking up an extra fifteen minutes early.

I yawned as I passed Preston's room, and was surprised to see the door was open. I slowed down and peeked inside, but he wasn't there. What was my brother up to now?

"There you are, honey." My mom smiled at me as I walked into the kitchen. "I was just about to send Preston in to wake you up, so you wouldn't be late."

I looked toward the table and saw Pres shoving a bite of toast into his mouth. His teasing smile matched his mom's perfectly. "Give Charlie a break. We've all seen what she looks like without her beauty sleep. She needs all the extra time she can get."

I rolled my eyes and sat down across from him. As soon as my butt hit the chair, a plate full of bacon and eggs magically appeared in front of me. "Thanks, Mom."

"You're welcome, honey."

I eyed my brother suspiciously. "Why are you up so early?"

My brother took another bite, not caring his mouth was full of food as he spoke. "Me and some of the guys are getting together to drill."

I raised a brow. "On a Saturday morning?"

Preston nodded as he swallowed.

"At seven?"

"Why is that so hard to believe?"

I set my hands on the table and fixed Preston with a stare. "Um, because I've lived with you for the last eleven years, and I've never seen you get up early unless you absolutely had to."

"It's senior year," he said.

"And you need to beat Brooks." It wasn't a question, and I hoped Preston wouldn't pick up on the lack of appropriate animosity in my tone. My face heated knowing I harbored a secret crush on his sworn enemy.

I turned my face down at my plate of food, afraid that he or our mom, who'd just sat down at the table with us, would notice my guilty expression.

"Wow. You must have really needed that sleep because you look super out of it," Preston said.

I kept my head turned down toward the table.

"No," Mom added. "She's probably just hungry. Charlie was supposed to get up early to eat—not argue with her brother."

She slid the plate closer to me, and I reached down to grab a piece of bacon. It settled as a giant lump in my stomach, but I plastered a smile on my face. "It's perfect."

Satisfied, our mom got back up and started washing some of the dishes she'd dirtied making breakfast. I looked up at Preston. "Ok, but seriously, why are you and the guys practicing so early? Not everyone has a super-vendetta against Brooks and feels the need to spend every waking moment gearing up to bring him down."

"Well, they should," he teased, and I forced a small chuckle. "One of the guys has work later this afternoon. We want to make sure we're a well-oiled machine this season."

I tilted my head and thought about their team's center. He had more dedication than the rest of the starting five put together, even if you took Preston's grudge into account. "You mean Mackey wants you to be a well-oiled machine, right?"

Preston leaned over the table so that his face was close to mine. "If we're all parts in the same machine. We all want that."

"You sound like you've been brainwashed."

His face went impossibly blank, his eyes stared off into the distance. "Join us, Charlie. Feed the machine."

I leaned over the table and playfully shoved his face. Preston just laughed as he stuck another bite of food into his mouth.

I let out a breath as I relaxed just a little. Teasing my brother was much more natural than keeping secrets from him.

"Don't you need to get going?" our mom asked a couple of minutes, and several bites, later.

I looked down at my phone. Helping Hands expected me at the nursing home in ten minutes, and it would take every one of them to get there in time. I'd been too busy thinking about Jackson, goofing around with Preston, and shoveling food into my mouth. I'd completely lost track of time. "Crap!"

I jumped up and grabbed my keys from the hook by the door.

"What are you doing?" Preston asked.

"I need the car."

"Uh, so do I."

Oh, right. My brother had an unofficial practice with his teammates. He'd literally just told me that.

"Come on," he said, already making his way out of the kitchen toward the front door. "I'll drop you off on the way to Mackey's."

"Yeah, but how am I gonna get home?"

He groaned. "I guess I'll have to pick you up, but shouldn't we get going?"

I looked back down at my phone. Nine minutes until Mrs. Gibbs had my head on a platter. I doubted talking to her nephew all week would earn me any special treatment.

"Good point. We'll figure it out on the way."

Preston and I raced out the front door, as our mom yelled at us to drive safely. "Helping Hands isn't worth getting into an accident! Neither is your practice, Pres!"

Laughing at Mom's overprotectiveness, we quickly got in the car, and my brother backed out of the driveway.

He took each speed limit sign we passed as a mere suggestion, which meant we pulled up to the front door of the nursing home with one minute to spare.

"Thanks, Pres" I yelled as I jumped out of my seat. "I'll text you later when I need a ride."

"Whatever," he said as I slammed the door.

I ran to the front door and skidded to a stop when I joined the rest of the group in the lobby.

"You're late," Mrs. Gibbs said the moment I joined them.

I shook my head. "No, I still have a minute."

She looked down at her watch and back up to me with a frown but didn't say anything else about it. Instead, she started talking to the group about the kind of behavior that was expected while we were here. We were to use "sir" and "ma'am" when we talked to all the residents. Our job was to help with small tasks they were unable to do, but if the residents we were assigned to wanted to talk, we were to slow down and spend some time listening.

"Some of these people don't get a lot of visitors. We want to make sure we make them feel valued."

She continued to go over the rules, and I looked around at the group. I'd only seen these people sweating up a storm as we picked up trash and cleaned up Saunders Park. I had to admit, the other delinquents and I cleaned up nicely.

Most of the girls wore dresses, though there were a couple of them who wore dress pants like me. The guys were in button-down shirts and khakis, and all looked very handsome. My eyes continued to scan the crowd, but I couldn't find the one person I was looking for.

Mrs. Gibbs started assigning places for everyone and paired me with the girl who had warned me about Jackson the week before. I now knew her name was Mila. She wore a dress covered in flowers that were almost as small and petite as her. She watched me as I walked over to her with a look that wasn't exactly cold but wasn't warm either.

"Looks like we're partners," I said as I stood beside her.

She lifted her eyebrows. "Yep."

"Our first room is in the East wing."

"Uh, huh."

Apparently, she wasn't the talkative type. That was fine.

When we arrived at the first room, we helped move some things around for all of five minutes before the elderly woman had us sitting down and looking at photo albums. We ooh-ed and ahh-ed at the appropriate times and before I realized it, an entire hour had passed.

"Um," I interrupted a long-winded monologue about the Vietnam war. "We need to go help some other women with their rooms."

A small smile touched Mila's lips—the first one all morning—but she still didn't say anything.

The woman let us go without much of a fight, and soon we were standing in the hallway ready to start all over again. At this rate, we'd move some picture frames in about five rooms, if we were lucky. But at least it wasn't picking up trash in the sun again.

I was just lifting my hand to knock on the next door when a male voice called out down the hall. "Hey!"

I looked over to see Jackson walking in our direction. My stomach flipped at the sight of him. He wore a crisp white shirt, a straight tie, and a pair of black pants. His brown hair was neatly combed back.

That boy could pull off the well-dressed look as well as he managed to look good while working outside in shorts and a tee.

I couldn't stop the sigh that escaped my lips, and when Mila turned her head sharply in my direction, I knew she'd heard it too. She'd literally been warning me about Brooks the week before, and now I was practically turning into a puddle as he got closer.

"Mila," he said as he stopped in front of us.

"Brooks." Mila crossed her arms across her chest.

Jackson's posture was stiff.

I felt like I'd just walked in on an argument of some sorts, even though Jackson was the one to step up to us.

There was a history here, and it wasn't a pleasant one. Had I been spending the morning with his ex-girlfriend? Was that the reason she'd been so quick to discourage my flirting? Or why she'd been quiet all morning?

"Would you mind giving us a minute?" he asked Mila.

She gave me one more of her mysterious looks, but eventually nodded and walked down the hall away from our assigned room.

Once she was safely out of range, I looked up at Jackson, a giddy smile on my lips. "Hey."

He smiled in return. "Hey."

"I didn't see you this morning. You know, in the group in the lobby." My voice trailed off, realizing how lame and stalker-ish I sounded.

But thankfully, Jackson's smile only grew.

"Yeah, I missed you too." He winked.

"That's not what I was saying!" I argued.

Jackson chuckled. "You were worried you weren't going to see me today. Admit it."

"No," I said, sure my cheeks were bright red but unwilling to tell him I'd been looking for him.

"Fine. I'll admit it then. I was afraid I wasn't going to see you today. Aunt Kathy had me helping the guys who work here by bringing in some boxes from this morning's delivery. It was unbelievable how many of them there were."

"I wonder why," I mused aloud, trying not to picture Jackson's muscles flexing as he moved box after box.

"It was mostly food." He leaned in close and whispered. "You wouldn't believe the amount of Jell-O the people who live here eat."

"Really?"

He nodded seriously. "It's like liquid gold to these people."

"Or gelatinous gold, in this case."

"Exactly."

We stood in silence and, once again, I was taken aback by how handsome he looked all dressed up. I wondered what it would be like to go to the dance that night with him, and like a complete idiot blurted, "Tonight is Rosemark's Homecoming."

As soon as I spoke the words, I regretted them. The

blush was back, and I swore I could feel it creeping all the way down my neck. I closed my eyes.

Please don't make a big deal out of this, I thought to myself as I waited for him to respond.

When he didn't speak, I slowly opened my eyes and was met with him staring intently at me. A crease formed between his brows. His mouth opened like he was going to say something, but he quickly closed it.

"Yep," I said. "And I'm going to go crawl into a hole now."

I started to turn to find Mila because even her creepy silence was sounding better than this, but Jackson reached out and grabbed my wrist.

"Don't go."

I stopped and faced him. My skin burned where he touched me.

His gaze was questioning. "I'm just not sure what you're trying to say. Are you asking me to go to your Homecoming with you tonight?"

I let out a weird, strangled sound from the back of my throat and shook my head back and forth quickly. Just because I imagined it, didn't mean I was asking for it. "No," I said emphatically and tacked on some more for good measure. "No, no, no, no, no."

Jackson let out a breath of relief and smiled. "Phew. I was trying to figure out how I was going to survive the lion's den."

"Wait. Would you have said yes?" I looked down to where he still held onto me.

"I don't know." He paused. "Maybe?"

Huh. That was unexpected.

"Are you going?" he asked.

"Nope." I lifted my shoulders. "My ex is going to be there, and I don't want to risk bumping into him."

"That guy's pretty bad, isn't he?"

"Yeah." I glanced down at my shoes, not wanting to talk about Anderson. I changed the subject. "So, what are you supposed to be doing right now?

He looked up and down the hall. "Oh, yeah. Well, my Aunt Kathy told me I could take a little break before I unload a few more boxes."

"Then you should go. I don't want you to get in trouble." I reached out and pushed his shoulder. My hand found strong muscle.

Jackson looked down to where my hand touched him, and I quickly pulled it back.

"I'm glad I found you, you know."

I lifted my brows. "Oh, yeah? Why's that?"

"Because as pretty as you were picking up trash, you're even prettier all dressed up."

My breath caught in my chest. Unable to answer, I smiled and tucked an imaginary strand of hair behind my ear.

"Jackson!"

We both looked toward the direction of the voice. Mrs. Gibbs sped down the hallway. "I've been looking all over for you. I told the owner of this place you'd be helping with some of the larger boxes, and then you went completely MIA."

Jackson didn't move immediately, so she lightly patted his back. "Go on, now."

Jackson walked down the hall, and I really tried not to admire the way he looked in his pants.

"And you." The smile fell from my face as I turned back toward Mrs. Gibbs. She wore a mask of disapproval, probably because she'd just caught me checking out her nephew. "You're supposed to be helping some of the female residents. Where's Mila?"

"I, uh..."

"Go find her and get back to work."

"Yes, ma'am."

I walked down the hall looking for Mila. I was prepared to search all over the nursing home, but she found me as soon as I turned the corner.

"Don't say I didn't warn you," she said before we started back on that day's activities.

CHAPTER EIGHT

6:03 PM

Daria: Are you sure I can't convince you to come to Homecoming with me????

Charlie: Uhhhh... Aren't you going to dinner soon?

Daria: You could throw on a dress and some lipstick in like 5 minutes.

Charlie: As appealing as rushing to get dressed up sounds, I do NOT want to see Anderson all over Linzie. Sorry. I'm staying in.

Daria: You stink.

Charlie: Not as bad as you do after basketball practice.

Daria: Oh, whatever. You're talking trash now, but just you wait until tryouts next week. This stinky girl is gonna leave you in her dust.

Charlie: You wish!

Daria: Hey, gotta go. My mom is downstairs yelling about pictures.

Charlie: Have fun!

Daria: Text me if you change your mind.

Nope. I had big plans that involved doing absolutely nothing. There was nothing that was going to change my mind.

Charlie: Sorry. Not happening!

I'd no sooner set my phone down when a knock came at my door.

"Come in," I answered, and Preston opened the door.

My brother made a show of doing a weird dance-turn move that could have rivaled the late Michael Jackson. "What do you think?" He tugged at the lapels of his grey suit jacket. He looked good, not that I had any intention of feeding his ego. I looked at his flower-covered tie and raised my brows.

His eyes went to where my gaze lingered, and he shrugged. "Beth picked it out. She said it matches her dress."

I shook my head and laughed. "That girl has got you wrapped around her fingers."

Preston chuckled. "Have you seen her, Charlie? Of course, I want to be wrapped around her fingers."

"You're hopeless."

He straightened his posture and pushed his shoulders back. "I'm not hopeless, I'm romantic. There's a difference."

"If you say so." I rolled my eyes.

"As your older, and much wiser, brother, I'm going to have to stick to my guns on this one."

I pantomimed wrapping a string around my finger.

Preston shook his head. "Listen, everyone's gonna be here soon, but Mom wanted me to check on you. You know, make sure you were okay not going to Homecoming since it's senior year and all."

I rubbed my palm over my forehead. "Why does everyone keep saying that?"

Preston looked at me, confusion evident on his face.

I pointed to where my phone sat on my bed. "I literally just got done having this conversation with Daria."

"Ah."

"Yeah." I nodded. "Anderson will be there tonight, and while I have no desire to get back together with him, I also don't want to throw up all over the dance floor from watching him and Linzie dance all up in each other's business."

"Because that's worse than the making out all over Rosemark?" he asked.

He, of course, was referring to the way Anderson acted around Linzie. He'd finally accepted we weren't getting back together and had been kissing the girl all over campus like it was the secret to curing cancer or something.

There wasn't a student at Rosemark who hadn't caught

them swapping spit in the hallways, or the lunchroom, or the parking lot. No place was safe!

"I don't know. I'd prefer not to see any of it." I shook my head to clear the images. "Plus, it's just a dance. There'll be another one in the spring. Maybe by then, I'll be up for dressing up and dancing. Who knows, I might even find a respectable guy to take me."

Like Jackson, I thought to myself.

"Oh, please. We both know I'm the only worthwhile guy at Rosemark, and I'm your brother, Charlie. Stop being so weird."

With those words, all gushy feelings about Jackson went right out the window. I laughed and threw my pillow at Preston. "Right. Because I'm the weird one."

Preston beamed back at me before an earnest look came over his face. "Seriously, though. What are you going to do since everyone will be there?"

"Not everyone." I pointed at myself.

"You know what I mean."

I shrugged. "I don't know. Wear pajamas and watch TV? I'm not completely dependent on others. Contrary to popular belief, a night in won't kill me."

"I hope not." He gently smacked his hand against the door jamb. "Well, I guess have fun watching TV."

"And you have fun bending to Beth's every whim and make sure to tell her I said hi."

"Of course." Preston smiled at me one last time as he walked out.

The limo drove up several minutes later. I peeked out

my window and watched as several people from the team poured out and congregated on our front lawn. Jeremiah looked uncomfortable in his suit and tie, while a girl I didn't know very well stood next to him. I spotted Sammi in the crowd but was surprised Linzie wasn't connected to her hip—and thrilled when I noticed Anderson's absence too.

My mom soon joined them and made everyone pose in front of the limo. The girls lined up, each putting a hand on their hip, while the boys all stood straight with serious expressions on their faces. It was terribly cliché, and I was happy to be a spectator this year.

Unfortunately, I forgot I was being a bit of a peeping Tom when Sammi's gaze found my window. Her eyes narrowed as she realized I was watching her.

I quickly closed the curtain and fell to the ground and out of sight, but the damage was done. Within thirty minutes, everyone would know about creepy Charlie Royce and her voyeuristic tendencies.

Awesome. That was just what this day had been missing.

I stayed on my bed until the crowd outside silenced, and the sound of the vehicle they'd just crammed back into drove off. Now that they were gone, I could finally relax. I opened the top drawer looking for my favorite pajamas, ready to veg out like I'd told Preston I would, but a buzz from my phone had me picking it up instead.

6:41 PM
Romeo: What are you up to?

I smiled as Jackson's text lit up the screen. I took a picture of my flannel pajama set still folded in the drawer and hit send.

Charlie: Oh, you know. Very exciting plans.
Romeo: You're one fancy lady, Charlie.
Charlie: You know it.
Romeo: So, I was thinking about what you said.

I sent a string of question marks.

Romeo: Tonight is your Homecoming dance, and you don't get to go. Wanna come out with me instead?

I really was looking forward to a night in, but I was curious.

Charlie: Where are you going?
Romeo: Langford Farm for the haunted maze with some friends from school.
Charlie: I don't know.
Romeo: Come on! It'll be fun and I promise to keep you safe from all the ghosts.

The idea of Jackson keeping me safe was more than

just a little appealing. Turned out, there was one thing that could make me want to leave the house tonight.

Charlie: Let me see what I can do.
Romeo: We're meeting up there at 7:30.
Charlie: Ok.
Romeo: Text me if you come, so I'll know to look for you.

The text echoed his words that morning when he'd told me he was looking for me. It was sweet and incredibly refreshing to have a guy talk so openly.

I took a deep breath as I set my phone down. Yep. I wanted to go. I'd just need to convince my parents to let me.

Step one: dress the part.

I needed something cute and warm. Having lived in Marlowe Junction my entire life, the warm part wasn't a problem. My closet was filled with clothing to help me survive the cold temperatures. Unfortunately, the cute part wasn't as easy. I wasn't one of those girls who had a closet full of cutesy stuff—no puffy vest, no knee-high boots. I never joined in on Han Solo season that was so popular.

I rummaged through my clothing trying to find something that might work and finally settled on a pair of skinny jeans, a long-sleeve shirt, and my signature Chucks. Usually, I wore my letterman jacket, but that wouldn't work for tonight. Instead, I topped off my ensemble with a gray hoodie.

The girl who stared back at me in the mirror was nothing special, but at least she was me. Jackson would know exactly what he was getting when he saw me tonight.

Which brought me to step two: convince my parents to let me go.

I decided the best approach was to be honest with my parents and hope they'd be okay with my unexpected excursion.

When I walked out to the living room, both of my parents were already there. They were curled up on the couch together watching a movie. When they saw me, my mom and dad quickly broke apart like two teenagers caught making out in the movie theater. I barely kept the smirk from forming on my face.

"Hey, Charlie," my dad said leaning forward, so he was sitting up straighter than when I walked in.

"Dad," I responded sitting on the love seat that was perpendicular to the couch.

"What's up?"

"So, I was thinking, since I didn't go to Homecoming, maybe I could go out somewhere else for a little while tonight?"

My dad blinked several times. "Aren't your friends all at Homecoming?"

I wiped my hands on my thighs. "Well, not all of them."

My dad briefly turned to look at my mom before facing me once more. "I don't think I'm following you."

"I've been making..." I struggled for the right word for

Jackson. "...friends with some of the people at Helping Hands. A couple of them are going to Langford Farm tonight for the corn maze, and they invited me to go with them."

"Are you sure the kids from Helping Hands are the best people to be hanging out with?" my mom asked with a frown.

"Well, not everyone there is a troublemaker. Just think about me."

They both fixed me with a stare, and I realized that might not have been the best argument to lead with. I needed to redirect.

"And one kid volunteers there because his aunt is the director. That's the kind of thing that builds character." I nodded enthusiastically.

"I don't know, Charlie," Dad said. "I'd feel a lot better if Preston was there. Or even Daria."

"But they're at the dance. The one I couldn't go to after Anderson broke my heart." I gave them my best puppy eyes. If they didn't cave soon, my bag was going to run out of tricks.

"Charlie," my mom said with a sigh.

"I'll have my cell phone, and my own car. And it's not like there won't be other people there. There will be old-man Langford, and I'm sure families too. Please?" I put my palms together in front of my face.

My parents looked at each other, and appeared to have a silent conversation between themselves as they raised eyebrows and tilted their heads. My mom let out a long, audible breath, and dad turned to me.

"You can go."

I lit up. "Seriously?"

"Yes, but"—he lifted his finger—"I expect you to be home by ten."

That would give me a solid two hours at the corn maze with Jackson. And the best part was I didn't have to worry about bumping into any Rosemark students. I got up from the loveseat. "Okay."

"And if either of us texts you, you need to respond right away."

"Okay." I bounced on the balls of my feet.

"Have fun, Charlie," my dad said, but I was already grabbing my keys and walking out the door for my date with the enemy—and feeling way too excited about it.

CHAPTER NINE

HALF AN HOUR LATER, I was pulling up to Langford Farm. I quickly checked my appearance in the rearview mirror, turning my face this way and that. Even without makeup, I looked pretty good. My hair was smooth and shiny—my eyes bright with excitement. When I was satisfied nothing was hanging out of my nose, and nothing was stuck in my teeth, I got out and made my way toward the maze entrance.

There was a giant sign that had "Langford Farm Haunted Corn Maze" painted on it, but it wasn't necessary. The corn maze was legendary in Marlowe Junction. I still remembered the first time Preston and I were allowed to go. We'd been begging for years for our parents to take us, and every year they said no.

The first Halloween we were both thirteen, my dad sat us down and told us we were too old to go trick-or-treating anymore. Preston had groaned until Dad clarified that it meant we were now old enough to go to the haunted maze.

We screamed the whole time, and I was pretty sure I had nightmares for a month, but we'd both felt so grown up. Preston and I had gone together ever since, until this year. He'd wanted to go with Beth instead, and I was planning on going with Anderson at some point, though we'd never settled on a day.

Now I was meeting Jackson and his friends. It was weird how much could change in just a few short weeks. I looked around for the guy in question. When I didn't see him right away, I walked over to where old Mrs. Langford sold tickets for the haunted maze. I paid for one, and she handed me a map of the maze.

Every year, the people at Langford Farm chose a different design to etch out in their cornfield. From popular movies and TV shows to seasonal shapes, it was always exciting to see what they came up with.

This year, the maze was in the shape of a jack-o-lantern, which sounded boring at first. But as I looked closer at the small, postcard-sized map, I could see there were just as many twists and turns as previous years—and I was sure just as many people waiting in the shadows to jump out and scare unsuspecting victims.

"Boo!" a voice yelled in my ear as a hand settled on my shoulder.

I jumped and screamed, dropping the map of the jack-o-lantern maze on the ground. Jackson laughed as I turned to face him. I gave him a quick shove before bending over and grabbing the paper that had fallen from my hands.

"Not funny," I said giving him an angry look that we both knew was all for show.

A corner of his mouth lifted. "It was pretty funny."

I grumbled under my breath as I shoved my hands into my pockets, crinkling the map in the process. "Whatever."

"Oh, don't be embarrassed. I was just playing around. Besides, I got you something."

I noticed he held one hand behind his back awkwardly and lifted my brows. "Oh, yeah?"

"Yep." Jackson pulled his hand around, and in it was a small, plastic container. Inside that was a corsage. It consisted of a couple of delicate white roses, with green and orange ribbons fashioned into bows.

Rosemark's school colors.

I looked at him, as a hesitant smiled formed. "What is this?"

He opened the container and pulled out the corsage. It was the kind that went on your wrist, so I stuck my hand out. Jackson stretched the bracelet part of it and put it on me.

"It's your Homecoming tonight. I thought it might be nice to celebrate somehow." He leaned in, his voice low as he asked, "Do you like it?"

Jackson's nearness mixed with the scent of his cologne had a dizzying effect on me. Speechless, I nodded.

Jackson stepped back. "Good. Let's go introduce you to my friends."

His voice was cheery—not at all teasing—and I doubted he knew the effect he had on me. As he guided me to where a small group of kids our age stood, all of my attention zeroed in on where his hand gently touched my back.

None of his friends overtly looked in our direction as we walked up, but I could see the way they watched our every move from the corner of their eyes. Their posture was stiff and forced as they pretended not to notice Jackson bringing me over to them.

My stomach churned as we got closer to the group. I felt so out of my element here, and I wondered if I would have been better off staying home or even going to the dance. Not that those thoughts did me any good now that it was too late to change my mind.

"Hey, everyone," Jackson's voice rang out. "This is Charlie."

Several eyes went from Jackson to me, to the tacky corsage I wore on my left hand.

"Charlie, this is...everyone." He waved his hand at the people standing there.

I lifted my hand in a sad excuse for a wave. "Hey."

I waited for him to list off names, or for "everyone" to tell me who they were, but we just stood watching each other. Jackson might have been friends with all of us, but different social circles didn't always mesh well, and we were busy sizing one another up.

Jackson's friends consisted of two guys and a girl. One of the guys had spiky, blond hair and had his arm slung over the shoulder of a girl with fiery, red hair that rivaled Preston's. The other dude had dark hair similar in color to Jackson's. He had his arms crossed over his chest, and I wondered if it was just how he stood, or if he felt put out by my being there.

What did they see when they looked at me? A tomboy with a tacky corsage who ditched her own Homecoming to go to a corn maze with Jackson?

"So, you're the girl who's had Brooks all twisted up these last few weeks," the girl said. Her voice was curious, and not at all unkind.

I looked down at the roses on my wrist. "Uh, I guess?"

She laughed. "Do you know we had to talk Brooks out of wearing a suit tonight?"

"Huh?"

"Yep." She nodded. "He thought it would be super cool to dress up like we were going to Homecoming, even though ours was last week. Something about making tonight special."

The blond guy who had his arm over her shoulder choked on a laugh, and I managed to sneak a glance in Jackson's direction.

He cleared his throat and shook his head. "Thanks, Annabelle."

Annabelle shrugged. "Just telling her like it is. The way you were practically bursting with excitement on the way here makes me think she must be pretty amazing."

Jackson ran a hand through his hair. "And, once again, I gotta thank you for helping me play it cool."

"Like anyone thinks you're cool," spiky-haired guy said.

Annabelle looked up at him. Her tone took on a playful quality. "Brooks thinks he's like, totally awesome and junk."

They laughed, even causing Mr. Quiet who stood off to the side to grin.

My own laugh surfaced, which caused Jackson's head to snap in my direction. I smiled sheepishly at him. "Sorry, but your friends are hilarious."

"Are you kidding me? Don't apologize. I'm glad you like them. I just wished it wasn't at my expense."

The guy with the spiky, blond hair spoke up. "Aw, poor Brooks and his wounded pride. Whatever will you do?"

I didn't know what I'd expected from Pinebrook kids. A bunch of people who kicked puppies and took candy from little kids? But the way they ripped on Jackson made me think of how my teammates and I acted toward one another.

I let out another giggle.

"And now she's laughing at me." Jackson threw his hands up in the air. "I hope you're all pleased with yourselves."

"Just positively giddy," Annabelle replied.

Jackson let out a long breath. "Why don't we just get our tickets and go inside?"

His friends all chuckled as they walked over to where Mrs. Langford stood to buy their tickets. Jackson put his hand on my arm to hold me back.

"I wish you would have waited to let me buy your ticket."

"I wasn't sure if this was a..." I hesitated to say the last word.

"A date?"

I nodded. "Yeah. Or if we were just hanging out."

"No way, this is definitely a date. And hopefully a good one."

I gave him a playful smile. "The jury's still out on it."

"Looks like my friends have turned you against me."

"Like I said, I think they're great."

"They aren't that great. It doesn't look like they're waiting for us." He pointed to where they disappeared through the entrance of the corn maze. "Should we go try to catch up?"

"Sure."

As we started walking, he reached down and grabbed my hand. My steps faltered, and my gaze went to where our fingers intertwined. When I managed to look back up at him, he asked, "Is that okay?"

I nodded, too afraid to speak, but charged with excitement.

"Cool."

Yeah, cool, except the place where our hands met had me feeling anything but. I felt flushed all of a sudden and I worried my hand was clammy in his. I was like a little girl with her first boyfriend, even though I was seventeen and had dated plenty in my high school days.

As we neared the entrance of the maze, the sound of

crows cawing over the giant speakers became louder. The accompanying music sounded like it might have been an organ. It had to be some kind of "spooky sounds" CD they'd found in the dollar bin. It wasn't scary, just annoyingly loud.

I couldn't wait until we made it inside the cornfield. The tall stalks helped filter some of the intensity of the sound. Jackson pulled a small flashlight from his jacket pocket and handed it to me, before reaching in again and grabbing another one. Thank goodness he'd brought two. In all my excitement to get out the door that night, I'd completely forgotten to bring my own.

We turned them on, and the small beams of light lit up the dark path. We walked in a straight line for several feet before we hit our first fork.

"Left, or right?" Jackson asked as he squeezed my hand.

"Uh..." I shrugged.

"You seemed to be staring pretty intently at the map when we showed up. I figured you were committing it to memory."

I pulled the wrinkled paper from my pocket. Even with the beam of light coming from the flashlight, it was hard to tell which direction we should go. "Left?"

"Okay." He pulled me down the path I'd suggested, without even double checking.

"Do you want to look at the map?"

"Nah, I trust you."

I stopped. "You shouldn't. I might be sending us

straight up the nose of the jack-o-lantern. Then we'd really have a hard time finding our way out."

He shrugged. "Then that means I get to spend more time with you."

"And as great as that sounds, I have to be home by ten."

Hot or not, he wasn't worth getting into more trouble for.

"That's like two hours from now. If we're still stuck in the maze then, I think we will have bigger problems than your curfew." He shot me a wink that made my knees weak.

Okay, maybe he *was* worth getting in trouble for.

We started walking again, as I tried to calm my heart. "You're probably right."

"Of course I'm—"

"Braaaaains!"

"Ahhhh!" I yelled and leaned into Jackson, as a woman dressed as a zombie jumped out from the stalks. My heart continued to beat frantically beneath my ribs, and I told myself it was more from getting startled than the way his chest rumbled as he laughed at my reaction.

Oh, who was I kidding? It was like ninety-nine-percent Jackson and one-percent the zombie.

"It's okay. I got you." He pulled his hand away from mine and wrapped it over my shoulder.

I wanted to tell him I wasn't scared, and I didn't need his protection, but the truth was I'd screamed like a little girl twice since meeting up with him. And even if I wasn't a scaredy-cat, I liked the way his arm felt draped over me.

He was just tall enough that it fit comfortably as we walked side-by-side.

I thought of all the times I had to do an awkward shuffle when Anderson tried to walk like this with me.

Walking with Jackson was...nice.

We were met with fork after fork, and each time Jackson asked me which way to go. I chose without looking at the map, and soon we ended up in a dead-end. There were a couple of plastic arms and legs in a pile with fake blood poured over them. It looked like something you'd see in a low-budget horror flick our parents would have watched when they were kids.

I looked back up at Jackson. "Sorry."

He squeezed his arm tighter around me. "Like I said, I'm happy to spend the time with you."

"Why?" I asked without thinking.

"What do you mean?"

He pulled away so that he was facing me, but neither of us made a move to leave the dead-end.

I thought about all the things his friends said. How he was really into me. I lifted a shoulder. "It's just something Mila said."

He closed his eyes and nodded. "Of course, it was."

"Is she an ex-girlfriend?"

He let out a sigh, and I could see the small cloud his warm breath made in the night air. "She likes to think so."

"You know I don't know what that means."

"She's just had it in her head ever since she made the varsity cheerleading squad, that we were going to date. I think she wants to be the idyllic varsity basketball player and cheerleader power couple."

I laughed. "Wow."

"Yeah, and that's not what I want."

I took a deep breath. "So, what *do* you want?"

Jackson shrugged. "I don't know. I just saw you that first Saturday at Helping Hands, and I just couldn't stop watching you. You were so pretty, and I could already tell you weren't some prissy girl afraid to pick up trash. I begged my Aunt Kathy to let me work with you."

My eyes widened. "You said she sent you to keep an eye on me!"

"I didn't want to freak you out before I got a chance to talk to you."

"And do I need to be freaked out by you, Jackson?"

"I think you're good." He grinned. "But the real question is how scared should we be right now? We've been standing in this corner for several minutes, and nobody else has come down this way."

I looked down the path that led to where we'd been hanging out. Jackson was right. We hadn't seen any people dressed up as zombies or even anyone else who was navigating the haunted maze. I had no clue where we were thanks to randomly choosing right or left without any regard for the map they passed out. "Crap."

We were lost.

CHAPTER TEN

JACKSON PULLED out the folded-up map from his back pocket and shone his flashlight over the paper. "Yeah, I have no clue where we are."

I started laughing. "Has anyone gotten stuck in the maze before?"

"I don't think so?" He started walking down the path, still holding the map in his hands.

I quickened my stride to keep up with him. He turned left, so I followed him. When he turned right, I followed him again. Still, we didn't see anyone. It was creepier than someone covered in costume paint chasing us. And yet, I wasn't afraid. I had Jackson with me, and surely the Langfords wouldn't leave anyone in here overnight. There had to be some kind of protocol for people who never came out.

Right?

Jackson stopped and looked at the map again. He pointed to the stem at the top of the jack-o-lantern. "So, I think we're here. Which means if we go down there..." His voice trailed off as he walked down the path behind him. "We should—"

A guy jumped out and started yelling at us. Jackson reflexively reached for me, but it wasn't necessary. My eyes focused on our assailant, and I about lost it when I realized it was one of Jackson's friends. It was the guy with the spiky, blond hair who had teased Jackson when we'd stood together earlier. Now, he was bent at the waist laughing hysterically.

Jackson groaned. "Greyson."

"You should have seen your face, dude. You were so scared."

Jackson stood up straight. "I wasn't scared," he argued. "You just startled me."

"Whatever. That was freaking hilarious."

Annabelle came out from behind the corner. Her hand was covering her mouth as she also laughed at Jackson. "Greyson's right. That was pretty freaking hilarious. Where have you guys been?"

Jackson and I looked at each other, before he answered, "We got lost."

Annabelle's face scrunched up. "Really? This was like, the easiest haunted maze ever."

I raised my hand and spoke up. "It's my fault. Jackson let me navigate, and I had no clue where we were going."

Both Greyson and Annabelle's eyebrows went sky-high.

"Seriously?" Greyson asked. "I knew you were into her, but that's crazy."

Annabelle explained. "Brooks is super type A and is usually very controlling about the map."

I looked to Jackson, but he was busy shooting daggers in Annabelle and Greyson's direction.

"You should have seen him last year. He was the perfect troop leader making sure none of his little scouts got lost. It was super lame," Greyson added with a chuckle. "Annabelle and I were so excited to get to ditch him this year."

"Thanks, buddy," Jackson said, but not without good humor.

"Okay, but can we get out of here now?" Annabelle whined. "It's getting cold, and I am so ready for some hot apple cider."

Jackson and I followed Greyson and Annabelle out of the maze. The quiet guy from earlier stood under one of the giant, portable space heaters that were set up near the exit of the labyrinth. In his hand was a Styrofoam cup. He spoke to a couple of other people I hadn't seen earlier, but one wore a Pinebrook letterman jacket.

Jackson leaned in, his breath warm against my cheek. "Just so you know, I'm buying your cider. That way we can call this an official date."

I smiled up at him. "Sure thing," I answered. "But just so you know, that means I'm going to hang out near the heaters and beg your friends to tell me all the embarrassing stories they know about you."

His eyes narrowed. "You wouldn't."

"It's a done deal. Better get in that line before it gets too long." I winked for good measure, which earned a smile in return.

Jackson and Greyson walked over to where everyone stood waiting for cider, while Annabelle and I walked toward everyone else. Now that I was separated from Jackson, I felt totally awkward. It was one thing to stand in their presence and joke around when Jackson was by my side but faced with the reality of talking to his closest friends was absolutely terrifying.

Thankfully, Annabelle was super friendly the entire time, and Jackson returned within a few minutes. My shoulders relaxed as he handed me my drink.

"Thanks," I said as I lifted the drink to my face, allowing the steam to warm my skin. The stray looks from his friends didn't escape my notice, but they didn't seem to affect Jackson.

That, or he didn't care.

He took a sip from his drink, and quickly pulled the cup away from his mouth. "Whoa. I think they have the temperature set to boiling lava hot. Careful."

I rolled my eyes and took a sip because I wasn't a toddler, and I didn't need some boy telling me to be careful —no matter how cute or sweet he was. I instantly regretted my decision as I burned my tongue on the liquid that Jackson had accurately described when he called it lava hot.

Jackson smirked at me as I pulled my cup down as

quickly as he had and struggled to swallow the cider. "Told you it was boiling."

"Whatever."

Jackson leaned in close. "You're cute when you're trying to act tough, did you know that?"

I rolled my eyes. "And you look stupid when you patronize me."

Jackson's responding laughter drew everyone's attention again. He put his hand on my back and led me a few feet further from where his friends were—just out of earshot. He gave a quick look in the direction of the small group, before he said, "I had a really good time tonight."

I smiled up at him. "Me too."

Jackson cleared his throat, as he rubbed his cheek. "I'd like to go out with you again. Maybe just the two of us on a real date. What do you think?"

I hesitated.

Of course, I wanted to go on another date with Jackson. Walking through the corn maze with him had been a lot of fun, and it had been easy to forget just how intense the rivalry between him and Preston was. But Basketball season was just around the corner, and I knew the conflict between them would only get stronger.

How could I date a guy who my brother hated enough to skip school over? How could I date a guy who would be intentionally trying to take my brother down in every game they played against each other? Jackson went to Pinebrook for goodness sake! It would never work, and I would just end up with another broken heart when it was all over.

I took a deep breath and released it slowly. "I..."

I paused as I tried to figure out the best way to explain everything, but Jackson didn't give me a chance to finish my thought. "You know what? Don't answer yet, because I know what you're going to say, and I'm kinda hoping you might change your mind."

I bit my bottom lip. "Jackson."

"Charlie."

I let my lip slide from the hold my teeth had on it and smiled. "Fine. I'll think about it. But don't hold your breath, Romeo. We both know star-crossed relationships always end in tragedy."

Jackson shook his head. "But we're not star-crossed. We just go to different schools. That's not even a big deal."

I lifted my brows.

"Well, it won't be in seven or eight months."

"Assuming we even make it that long," I argued. "You're talking about what happens when summer rolls around, but we just had our first date."

Jackson ran his hand through his hair. "You're right, and I probably seem like such a hopeless romantic. I just really like spending time with you, and I'm not ready for it to be over, not when you seem to be having fun too."

I was having fun but didn't think I could say the words aloud. So I pulled out my phone and looked at the screen. It wasn't quite time for me to leave, but I decided to make my exit anyway. "I gotta go. And I'll think about it, okay?"

He smiled once more and stuck his hands into his pockets. "I'll take it, Charlie Royce."

"Goodnight, Jackson Brooks."

I walked out to my car by myself, sent a quick text to my parents letting them know I was on my way home and tried not to think about how bad I had it for Jackson.

Because if the flutters in my stomach were any indication, I was in deep trouble.

"HOW WAS THE CORN MAZE, CHARLIE?" my dad asked as I walked in the door, with thirty minutes to spare.

He and my mom were still sitting on the sofa—though there were a solid two feet between them this time. I wondered if they kept the PDA to a minimum for Preston and me, but it wasn't necessary.

We both were happy that our parents had found one another.

I shrugged as I stopped in the living room. "It was fun."

"Did you guys stay out of trouble?"

I thought about how Jackson was the perfect gentleman the entire time, and how even his friends were pretty tame. "Yeah, we just did the corn maze, got some cider and then I came home."

"And, do you feel better about not going to Homecoming now?" my mom asked.

"Yeah." I nodded as I answered honestly. "But, um, would you guys mind not telling Pres?"

I wasn't ready to answer his questions—specifically the one about who I went with.

I could see the concern in my parents' eyes.

"Everything is fine, and I swear I didn't do anything wrong. I just don't feel like going through a bunch of over-protective big brother questions."

A knowing smile touched my mom's lips. "There's a boy, isn't there?"

My face heated, thinking about Jackson.

"Wait." My dad sat up. "There's a boy?" He turned to my mom. "And you knew?"

She rested a hand on his shoulder. "Calm down. I didn't suspect anything until just now."

"It was a group," I quickly added. "It's not like it was a date, date."

Unless you asked Jackson.

"What's his name, his date of birth, his social security number? I'm going to need it all," my dad lifted a finger with each thing he listed off.

I snorted. "You didn't ask for all of that with Anderson."

"Yeah, and he turned out to be a terrible guy. Now, I know I have to do a little dad-recon."

I rolled my eyes. My dad was great, but he wasn't scary. His attempt at intimidating father wouldn't turn away anyone.

"But, really, a name would be nice," Mom said. Her voice was kind and filled with genuine curiosity.

"Jackson."

"And do we know this Jackson?"

Yep. He's just your son's biggest rival on the court, I thought, but couldn't say it. I quickly racked my brain for a good response when headlights shone through our front window. My brother was home.

I gave my parents a wide-eyed look. "I gotta go get changed. Please don't tell him."

"We won't," my dad assured me. "But don't think this is our last conversation about this Jackson boy you met up with tonight."

"Okay, okay."

I quickly went to my room and got dressed in my pajamas in record time. I listened as Preston walked through the front door and our parents gave him the third degree. It didn't matter if they were doing it for their benefit or mine, because regardless, it gave me just enough time to jump in my bed and pull up Netflix on my laptop before he gently knocked on my door.

"Charlie, you up?"

"Yeah, come in."

He walked in and sat down at the small chair I had in the corner of my room. "Geez, sis. Did you even leave your room?"

I didn't want to lie, so I settled on a shrug. How Preston interpreted it was up to him. "Did you have fun with Beth?"

He quickly looked down at the floor, but not before I saw the grin break out across his face.

"Please tell me you actually made it to the dance."

Preston's head snapped up. "Of course, I did. Beth and I danced the entire time."

"You know what?" I shook my head. "I don't even want

to think about my brother and his girlfriend and what they may or may not have been doing on the dance floor."

He barked out a laugh. "It was tame. You know Mr. Richards and his twelve-inch rule."

Oh, yes. It was notorious. He literally carried a ruler around the gym and held it up to couples who were getting too cozy during the slow dances. The third time he had to speak to someone, they were officially kicked out of the school dance.

"Wanna hear something weird?" he asked, his voice turning serious.

My breathing hitched, and I forced my fingers from fidgeting. Did Preston somehow know where I'd been that night?

"Always," I answered and hoped my voice was light.

"I didn't see Anderson the whole night."

I let out a breath. "That is weird."

"I was sure he would be there with Linzie, making a big show of it. But nobody saw either of them all night."

"Is it too optimistic to hope he finally realized what a d-bag he was being? And that parading his home-wrecker of a girlfriend at the Homecoming dance was a bad idea?"

Preston fixed me with a stare.

"Yeah, you're right."

We sat in silence for a few moments.

"Are you gonna be okay, Charlie?" Preston asked, breaking the stillness of the room. "You know, with this whole Anderson thing? I hate to think of you avoiding every school function because you don't want to bump into your ex."

"Don't worry about Anderson and me. After this, I promise it won't be an issue."

He watched me and eventually nodded. "Okay. I'm going to go to bed then. Dancing all night can really wear you out."

"Good night."

I shut my laptop now that I was done putting on a show for my brother and grabbed my phone from where it had fallen on the ground in my hurry to get dressed. Thankfully, Jackson hadn't messaged while Preston was in here.

Unfortunately, I had missed a text from someone else.

9:58 PM

Anderson: I know where you were tonight.

Charlie: What are you talking about?

He sent a picture of me standing with Jackson, Styrofoam cups in hands.

Crap, crap, crap.

It looked like I'd spoken too soon when I told my brother that Anderson wouldn't be a problem anymore. And the worst part? I couldn't go to Preston about it.

CHAPTER ELEVEN

PRESTON and I pulled up to Rosemark High together, but I hung back in the car until the bell was just about to ring. I leaned the passenger seat all the way back and lay there dreading the moment when I would have to talk to Anderson.

He hadn't texted me the rest of the weekend, but I knew it was coming. That was enough for a rock to settle deep down in my stomach on its own, but I also had the added stress of having tryouts later that day. Anderson couldn't have waited until tomorrow to mess with my head?

I looked down at my phone—three minutes until the tardy bell rang. I got out, slammed the door, and raced up to the school. I was just about to my homeroom when I felt a hand grab my arm.

"I was wondering if you'd ever show up since your brother walked in ages ago."

I turned to see Anderson standing behind me. I shook his hand off from where it held me. "I gotta get to class."

The corners lifted into what some might call a smile, but I could see the malice just beneath the surface.

"Anderson, the bell's gonna—"

Loud ringing interrupted my words, and I was still two doors down from where I needed to be. Maybe if I ran, my teacher wouldn't send me to the principal's office. Mr. Richards had told me I needed to be on my best behavior, and a tardy wasn't going to work in my favor.

"I'll talk to you later," I whispered harshly. "I can't be late."

"You're already late." He crossed his arms.

I turned from Anderson and started speed walking down the hall.

"Don't you walk away from me!"

"Is everything okay?" Mr. Richards seemed to materialize out of nowhere.

I let out an aggregated huff. Well, there was no way I was going to avoid getting in trouble now. Thanks, Anderson.

Anderson shot me a look, before putting a fake smile on. "No, sir. No problem."

I smiled and hoped it was convincing. As much as I hated being blackmailed by Anderson, I wanted to stay on his good side, and not give him any reason to go to Preston with the picture he took of me on Saturday night.

"Mr. Webb, why don't you go ahead and hurry to class. You can tell your teacher you were with me. If there's any question, I'll address it. Miss Royce, I'd like you to come with me to my office, please."

Mr. Richards started walking toward his office, not waiting to see if I would follow him. My future was held in his age-spot covered hands. Of course, I followed. I looked back at Anderson who watched me with raised brows. I shook my head, and I hoped he knew me well enough to know I wasn't going to snitch.

How had our roles reversed so quickly? In a matter of weeks, I'd gone from keying his car to cowering in fear.

With one last look at Anderson, I turned and followed Mr. Richards to his office. The walk was short and quiet, but my mind raced the entire time. Was he going to expel me? Was this the last straw before going to juvie? If that was the case, I planned to go out with a bang. I'd take all the anger I felt toward Anderson, and was unable to do anything with, and direct it toward Mr. Richards.

He sat down at his desk and motioned for me to sit across from him. I sat poised to attack, my heartbeat pounding in my ears.

"Are you okay?" he asked gently, leaning back in his seat.

"Huh?"

Mr. Richards closed his eyes and rubbed the bridge of his nose. "I've told you, Miss Royce. I'm not out to get you. It is my job to see that all of the students here feel safe— including you." He took a long breath. "Do I need to call Mr. Webb down here? Was he threatening you?"

"No," I answered, a little too quickly.

Mr. Richards watched me expectantly. I was sure he was waiting for me to rat Anderson out, but I wasn't going to do that. I couldn't even if I wanted to.

"Am I in trouble?" I asked when the silence stretched on.

My principal sighed, and I swore I saw a flash of disappointment in his eyes. "No, Charlie, not this time." He looked down at the oversized desk calendar in front of him. "Basketball tryouts are today."

I nodded.

"Good luck."

"Thanks?"

He scribbled a quick note on a yellow piece of paper. "Unless there's anything else you want to tell me, I think you'd better get to class."

I snatched the paper from his hands and walked out of his office without another word.

"WHAT IS WRONG WITH YOU?" Daria asked as we walked toward the gym after school.

I'd been quiet all day, and every time she tried to talk to me, I'd answered with one- or two-word responses. I shrugged. "Tryouts, I guess."

"Since when do you get worked up about basketball?"

"Since I have to explain to Coach Scruggs that I can't play for the first few games."

Daria snorted. "Yeah, good point."

Once we were inside the gym, and I immediately went

to Coach Scruggs to tell her about my predicament. She reacted exactly as I'd expected.

"I hope you're happy with yourself Royce," she said loud enough for everyone to hear. "You're my best point guard, and you're on athletic probation."

My face heated, and I looked down at my feet embarrassed. "I'm sorry Coach Scruggs."

She let out an angry puff of air, and I looked up to see a stern expression fill her face. "Don't apologize to me." She pointed to where my teammates stood. Most of them pretended not to be listening to our very loud interaction. "Apologize to them. When they don't have you in their first game, they are the ones who suffer."

She was right, and I kept my lips tightly pressed together.

"And don't think I'll be making you captain either. You're lucky I'm letting you try out at all."

"Yes, Coach Scruggs."

She shook her head, still upset with me. "Go join everyone else so we can begin."

I jogged over to where the rest of the girls stood. Daria wrapped her arm over my shoulder, and whispered, "At least that's done, and you can start acting normal now. And who knows? Maybe she'll change her mind about the whole captain thing."

I let out a long sigh and whispered back. "I don't know. She looks pretty angry, and she makes a good point. How can I lead a team I can't even play on?"

Daria rolled her eyes. "I took the liberty of looking up

this year's schedule. You only miss one week of games. There's practically a whole season ahead of you."

"Yeah, but—"

"If you ladies are done chit-chatting, I'd love to start our tryouts. You know, if that's okay with you, Charlie."

My face burned again.

"Everyone take two laps, and we'll go through some drills."

I slid a glance at Daria before running the perimeter of the court.

Still feeling the shame of my very public rebuke, I didn't run as quickly as I could. Several girls passed me as we moved just behind the basketball hoop. I got a few sympathetic looks, but I was careful to smile at everyone.

I might not make captain this year, but I still had a reputation on this team that I needed to maintain.

Coach had us start with ball handling. We dribbled up and down the court—left hand, right hand, crossovers, low. I caught a fresh-faced girl palming the ball, struggling not to look down as she dribbled down the court. She wasn't going to make the cut. Not with the girls we had this year, but it was great to see her determination. Maybe it would pay off in time for next year.

Coach blew her whistle. "Take five to get some water, and we'll move to passes."

Daria and I walked over to the side of the court and started drinking from our bottles.

"Good job out there," she said.

I tipped my chin at her. "You too."

"Wanna partner up for passes?"

"Obviously."

We took another minute to hydrate and walked over to where everyone stood forming two lines, facing one another. Coach had us starting with chest passes, then bounce passes. I watched everyone with a captain's eye, thankful to see no one had gotten rusty over the summer. It was an unfortunate part of playing on the high school team versus competitive leagues. So often, players got lazy over the summer and had to retrain their bodies. But it looked like everyone was pumped and ready for a good season this year.

When everyone started shooting drills, Coach called me over. I reluctantly jogged to where she stood watching everyone shoot free throws. Afraid of making things worse, I waited for her to speak. Thankfully, she wasted no time.

"We both know you have great aim, and I wanted to ask you what you thought about everyone."

I turned to face Coach Scruggs and raised my brows.

"No, I'm not making you captain. I need someone who can actually play." I let out a sigh. "But despite your hasty actions, I know you're dedicated to this team and want to see us at state your senior year."

I nodded. "Heck, yeah, I do."

"So, what would you be telling me right now if you *were* captain."

I watched as my soon-to-be teammates continued to throw the ball at the basket. With Coach's instruction, they moved from free throws to lay-ups to two-point shots.

As I stood there, I made my recommendations for the starting five. Obviously, Daria was my suggestion for center. She was perfect for the dirty work. I named people for shooting guards, and forwards. When it came time to tell Coach who I thought the point guard should be, I stumbled over my words.

I wanted to tell her me. I should be the point guard if circumstances were different, but what good would that do the team? I scanned the girls as they took turns at the basket. "Jasmine should do it."

Coach nodded. "I think you're right, Charlie. I've already decided to name her captain, but it's good to hear you can look at this objectively and not take it out on your teammates."

"Coach Scruggs. I would never!" I felt my blood boiling just beneath the surface. "If you think I would do that..." I trailed off and shook my head unable to finish the thought.

"Calm down, Royce. I'm making you co-captain."

"Wait. You are?"

Her lips were a thin line as she shook her head. "I can't deny your hustle and ability."

A grin broke out across my face.

"That doesn't mean you can walk all over Jasmine. It means you yield to her, you encourage her. Do you understand?"

I pressed my lips together to keep the smile from widening. This was the best news I could have gotten today. "Yes, ma'am."

"I'm serious, Charlie. Don't make me regret this."

"I won't."

She rolled her eyes. "Good. Now, get back out there and take a few shots before we break for the afternoon."

I did as she said, and before long, she was telling everyone to head home. "I'll post the team rosters tomorrow along with the captains for varsity and JV."

Everyone packed up, and Daria kept giving me funny looks until we walked out to the parking lot away from listening ears.

"So, what was that all about?" she asked as we neared our cars. Preston had agreed to get a ride with Jeremiah after school, so I could stay late for tryouts.

"What do you mean?" I answered nonchalantly, as I adjusted the bag that hung over my shoulder. While I couldn't wait to tell Daria the good news, I wanted to mess around with her a bit first.

What good was it to have a best friend, if you couldn't tease them a little?

She cleared her throat forcefully. "Obviously I'm asking what Coach said when she called you aside? Did she name you captain?"

I shook my head as I fought the smile that wanted to surface.

Daria drew her own conclusion and sighed. "That really stinks, Charlie. I'd kinda thought maybe she was going to find a way to make it work."

I let her words hang in the air just long enough to drive

it home before I added: "She said I could be co-captain though."

My friend looked at me, and when realization had completely dawned on her, she punched my arm. "Shut up! You are such a loser."

I laughed and rubbed the place where she hit me. Her punch was surprisingly hard, and I could feel the tenderness down to my muscle. "It's not official, so don't make a big deal out of it, okay?"

Daria stopped. "Um, hello? You are on athletic probation, and you still managed to get co-captain. I'd say that's a testament to how awesome you are."

"Maybe. I just need to make sure I'm on that court when the scouts come and watch us this year. It won't matter if I'm captain, co-captain, or the best high school athlete in the whole freaking country if I'm sitting on the bench."

We started walking again to where our cars were parked next to each other. Daria's pristine SUV made my car look like it belonged in an impound lot, but Preston and I had saved all summer to go in on it together. With two working parents, our jalopy was a luxury we never took for granted. It was freedom on four wheels.

"Well, I'm convinced that this year is going to be the best year ever. You broke ties with Anderson just in time. Now we can enjoy our senior year together."

I shook my head. "Whatever you say, Daria."

"I do say."

My phone buzzed, and I quickly looked at the screen.

3:59 PM

Romeo: How were tryouts?

I hadn't talked to him since our date at the haunted corn maze, but he'd still remembered how important today was.

"Who's that?"

"Nothing." I cleared my throat. "I mean, no one."

"Charlotte Royce, do not lie to me. Judging by the stupid smile on your face, that isn't no one. I'd say that is a very special someone."

I put the hand that held my phone behind my back.

Daria's eyes narrowed. "Have you been keeping secrets? Who is it?"

She took a step forward. I took a step back.

"You'd better tell me."

I shook my head. "It's nobody."

Daria lunged forward and reached for my phone, but I held it just out of reach. We went back and forth until she eventually ripped it from my hands.

"So, who do we have here?" Her eyes scanned the screen. "Romeo?"

I looked at her with a blank expression, mentally praising my choice of contact name.

"I don't know any Romeos."

I stayed silent.

"Oh, my goodness. This is a code name, isn't it?"

My face heated. "Don't make a big deal out of this."

She pointed her finger at me, her face filled with delight. "You have a secret boyfriend. Charlie!"

"He's not my boyfriend," I mumbled.

"How long has this been going on?"

"I told you, he's not my boyfriend. We've been on like, one date." One wonderful date that landed me in a heap of trouble.

"And yet, he knew you had tryouts today. Sounds like it's pretty serious. Romeo cares about his Juliet."

"Shut up."

"Want me to respond?" Her fingers wiggled just above the screen.

I reached out and grabbed my phone from her and shoved it into my pocket.

Daria crossed her arms over her chest. Now that the playfulness of playing tug-o-war over my phone had ended, she looked upset. "Why did you keep this from me?"

I shrugged. "It's not a big deal."

"Of course, it's a big deal. Wait, are you embarrassed by him?"

I shook my head. Embarrassed wasn't the right word. More like terrified of what Preston would say if he found out.

Her eyes widened. "Is he embarrassed by you? Please tell me you aren't dating someone who's in a relationship with someone else after what Anderson did to you."

"No! Daria, I wouldn't."

She raised her brows.

"Look, I'm sorry I didn't tell you. It just kinda

happened, and I'd just broken up with Anderson, and I didn't want to be that girl."

"What girl is that?"

"You know. The one who hops from boy to boy," I explained.

Daria snorted. "But you're not, and anyone who knows you, knows that."

"I guess I just didn't want to give anyone any more excuses to gossip about me, you know?

"Fine, I'll let you have that one, but don't think I'm going to drop it before you give me all the details." She paused. "Like, does Romeo go to Rosemark?"

I shook my head.

"Wait...don't tell me he goes to Pinebrook!"

I nodded.

"No wonder you named him that. You guys are star-crossed lovers like Romeo and Juliet."

I put my face in my hands. I guess this is what happens when you name your secret crush after a famous play.

"If you promise not to let your relationship end in some type of suicide pact, I'll allow it."

"Yeah, I already told him no daggers and no poison, so we should be good."

Daria's smile was sly. "Does Preston know?"

I shook my head frantically. "Please don't say anything, okay?"

"Whoa. Calm down. It's not like it's Brooks or anything."

How did she guess? I tried to keep my expression blank but knew I failed miserably.

Daria burst out in laughter. "Your face was priceless. Chill, Charlie. I know you're not that stupid."

I forced a chuckle. "Yeah, right?"

She shook her head. "You'll have to tell me more about lover boy later. I have to get home and finish reading *Madame Bovary*. I keep falling asleep every time I try, and our test is tomorrow."

"Have you tried reading the CliffsNotes?"

"Yeah, and they're just as bad." She blew me a kiss and opened her car door. "Talk to you later."

I gave a small wave. "Yeah, see ya."

She drove off, and I couldn't help but wonder how I was going to get out of the massive hole I kept digging for myself.

CHAPTER TWELVE

THE NEXT MORNING, Preston was a ball of nerves. He barely ate breakfast and drove like a maniac—even more so than usual. I thought I would tear the oh-crap handle from its spot above the passenger door on the way, but we made it to school alive.

Barely.

He turned to face me as we pulled into a spot. "Don't forget to get a ride home today, since I'll be staying late."

I stared at him blankly as I tried to figure out what the heck he was talking about.

"Because basketball tryouts are today." Preston sighed. "Please tell me you have a ride home today."

"Totally."

Preston shook his head. "Look, I know you made co-captain and all—"

"Wait, what? How did you hear that?" I shrieked. It hadn't been made official yet.

He shrugged. "Veronica, obviously. But now that you made your team, it's time for me to make mine. Senior Year Rematch is almost here, and I need to get my head in the game. I need you to find a ride home."

"I have a ride home today," I lied, fully intending to text Daria as soon as my brother was out of my sight. "I was just recovering from my life flashing before my eyes after you ran that red light."

"Oh, good." He paused. "And the light was yellow."

"In your dreams."

"Whatever. I'll see you later, okay?"

"Yeah, see ya," I answered, but he was already out of the car and on his way to the main building of the school.

I pulled out my phone and shot a quick text to Daria.

Charlie: Can you give me a ride after school?

She answered right away.

Daria: Can't. I have a dentist appointment right before lunch.

I audibly groaned.

Daria: Where are you by the way? You'd better not be hiding in your car.
Charlie: I'm not. Walking up to the school right now.

I reached down to grab my bag from the floor of the car.

Knock! Knock! Knock!

The angry banging on the car window had me jumping. I looked up to see Daria giving me a playful, stern look. She held her phone up and pointed to where I'd just texted her.

"You are a big, fat liar, Charlie Royce!" she yelled loud enough so that I could hear her through the window. Unfortunately, so did everyone else walking by.

I went to grab my bag a second time, and got out of the car, ignoring the curious looks of everyone walking by. "Good morning to you too," I said to Daria, who watched me in amusement.

"Okay, spill," she said as we walked up to the school.

"What do you want to know?"

"Charlie," she all but growled. "I swear you are the most irritating best friend in the history of best friends. I want to know all about..." she lowered her voice to a whisper. "Romeo."

Now, she chose to be quiet? After broadcasting I was a liar to everyone moments earlier? "There's not much to tell."

"Not much to tell? Girl, I saw the long stream of texts on your screen yesterday." My eyes widened. "And no, I didn't read them."

"Thank you."

"Ugh. I'm not that bad. But you gotta give me something since I'm keeping this a secret and all. Like, what's his real name."

She might not make the connection if I just gave her the first name. I hadn't. And it wasn't like his name was that uncommon, right? "Jackson."

"Jackson and Charlie, sitting in a tree, K-I-S-S—"

I smacked her. "Will you stop?"

She laughed. "Fine. So how did you meet him?"

"Marlowe Junction's Helping Hands."

"Your volunteer group?"

I nodded.

Daria waggled her eyebrows. "Is he a bad boy? Did he show up to the nursing home riding a motorcycle and wearing a black leather jacket? Does he have tattoos and smoke?"

"Don't be dumb."

"Fine. But I gotta know, is your totally-not-a-bad-boy hot?"

I thought of Jackson's green eyes and warm smile and nodded.

"I knew it!" She pointed an accusatory finger at me. "Have you seen him outside of Helping Hands?"

I played with the hem of my shirt and nodded again.

Her mouth fell open, and she smacked my arm. "Charlie! Are you kidding me? When?"

"Saturday night," I said behind a cough.

"Satur—" Her eyes went wide. "That's why you didn't want to come to Homecoming. Charlie, you brat."

"It wasn't like that."

Daria fixed me with a stare.

"I promise I planned to stay in that night. But then he messaged me after you and I texted, and he invited me to Langford Farm. So, I went." I shrugged.

"Did you kiss?"

The question wasn't out there. Daria and I had spent countless hours talking about the boys at our school and wondering what it would be like to kiss them. But I felt shy when it came to Jackson, and I wasn't sure if it was because I liked him so much or if it was because he was the enemy.

Maybe it was a combination of both.

I shook my head. "Of course we didn't. It was only our first date."

"But you wanted to, right?"

I couldn't stop the blush that heated my cheeks.

Daria started laughing. "Oh, man. My best friend's got it bad."

Yeah, she did.

Daria wrapped her arm around my shoulder as we walked in the front door of the school. "Here's the final question, Charlie." She paused and smiled deviously at me. "When do I get to meet him?"

Never.

I bit my lip and was mercifully saved from answering her question by the bustle of the hallway as everyone raced to class.

THE REST of the day went smoothly, and I'd completely

forgotten about finding a ride home from school until I walked out to the parking lot.

Crap. Crap. Crap.

Daria was gone. Preston was at tryouts. Mom and Dad were working. And from the look of things, the other people I usually would have asked had already high-tailed it out of school.

I could wait for my brother to finish tryouts, but then I'd have to admit I never got the ride I told him I had. My heart skipped as another option entered my mind. It was crazy and possibly worse than just asking Daria to come get me since she had to be done at the dentist by now.

But once the idea came, it wasn't easy to shake it. Part of me wondered what he would say, and I convinced myself that was the only reason I was choosing Jackson over my best friend.

I pulled out my phone.

2:05 PM

Charlie: What are you doing right now?????

Romeo: I just pulled into my driveway. Why?

Charlie: Oh. No reason.

Now that I knew he was already home, I felt silly asking him to come get me. Daria it was. I started to text her when another message from Jackson came through.

Romeo: Seriously. What do you need?

Charlie: I was going to ask if you would give me a ride home.

I held my breath and hit send before I could chicken out. His answer came immediately.

Romeo: From Rosemark?
Charlie: Yeah, my brother has basketball tryouts today.

The small bit of information felt too close to a betrayal, even though there was nothing Jackson could do with it.

Romeo: I'm like 10 minutes away. If you go out front, I'll just swing by.
Charlie: Thank you!
Romeo: Don't mention it.

Fifteen minutes later, a white Jeep stopped in front of the school. The passenger window rolled down, and Jackson hollered out, "Come on!"

I quickly looked around to see if anyone was watching. After the picture Anderson took at the corn maze, you'd think I would be more cautious. When I didn't see anyone lurking behind the building with their spy camera, I opened the door and hopped in.

I quickly told him which way to go.

"Thanks again," I said as Jackson turned onto Main. "I owe you one."

Jackson chuckled. "Then I'm thrilled I came to get you. Can't wait to cash that one in."

"Shut up." I rolled my eyes, even though he couldn't see me with his attention on the road.

"I'm serious. I already know what I'm going to ask for."

I shifted in my seat, so I faced him. "Oh, yeah? And what's that?"

"A second date."

I groaned.

"No, I'm serious. And if you hate it, I won't ask you again. I promise."

"What about Saturdays?"

He stole a quick glance in my direction, as I told him where to turn. "What about them?"

"Won't it be weird if we stop dating and then we still have a bunch of community service hours together?"

Jackson shrugged. "I'll take those weeks off. It's one of the perks of doing it as an actual volunteer and not a delinquent."

"Ouch, dude."

He chuckled, and I warmed to the sound. I loved the way his laughter rumbled deep in his chest and always sounded like it escaped—never like it was forced.

I pointed to my street and told him to turn down it. "I'm the third house on the right."

"You mean the one with the basketball hoop in the driveway? I never would have guessed."

I gave him a playful shove. "Think you can try to stop being a smart aleck for like, two seconds?"

"But, Charlie, I might die."

I suppressed a giggle. "You're worse off than I thought."

Jackson parked. "And you're still just as pretty. Even when you're wearing orange and green."

I looked down at my Rosemark class shirt I wore that day. "Should I start wearing blue and white?"

Pinebrook's school colors.

"That would make a statement."

But just what kind of message would it send? That I was a traitor to my own school? Besides, I didn't think Jackson actually wanted me to start wearing his school colors. That would be too weird.

We stayed in the car, both looking out the front windshield, not talking for several moments. The more I tried to play it cool next to Jackson, the more I was aware of his every movement. He shifted in his seat, then cleared his throat. I took a deep breath and made my best effort to calm my beating heart.

"So, uh...thanks for giving me a ride." I tucked my hair behind my ear, but a strand got stuck on my lips.

My fingers went to pull it off but were met with Jackson's warm hand. I stopped and looked up at the boy who'd come to get me after school. His face was close and serious as he brushed the stubborn piece away. "I really want to kiss you, Charlie."

Oh yeah, there was no way my heart was going to find its normal rhythm now. It pounded inside my chest, and I was sure Jackson would be able to feel its rapid beating from where his fingers lingered on my cheek.

"Uhh," I answered quite articulately as Jackson's eyes searched my own.

"I want to, but I'm not going to." He pulled his hand away and leaned back.

My body slumped, and I let out a loud sigh.

"I told you, I like you. Not kissing you right now is really hard, but when I finally kiss you, I want it to be because you and I both want to."

"Oh, I want to." The words were out before I realized it, and I slapped a hand over my mouth as my eyes went wide.

Jackson chuckled, and my face heated.

"You know what I mean," he said looking at the clock on his dash. "I gotta go, but I'd love it if you texted me later."

Wait. Did he just say love?

Get it together Royce.

I nodded, keeping my face neutral to hide the direction my thoughts had spiraled. "Okay."

I got out of the car and waved at Jackson before walking up to the house. He stayed parked on the street until I got inside.

My parents weren't home yet, so I had the house to myself. Once the front door was shut, I leaned back against it and squealed as loud as I could.

Jackson Brooks had almost kissed me!

Not only that, I would have let him.

If he wanted to wait until I was interested in dating him, he might just be getting his wish. I mentally listed off all the reasons there were to like him.

He volunteered because he wanted to.

He was romantic.

He was considerate.

He was hot. (That was an understatement and really could be on the list twice.)

Jackson Brooks was the whole package. What girl wouldn't be falling over herself to date such a catch?

Oh, right. The girl who was related to his biggest rival.

I had to consider what this would mean for my reputation at school, and my relationship with my brother. True, it wouldn't be easy convincing my friends at school that dating a guy from Pinebrook was no big deal, but it was something I'd be willing to do.

Preston, however, was a completely different story. I wasn't sure that he'd be able to look past who Jackson was, no matter how big of a romantic my brother could be.

Of course, if he cared about me at all, then he'd know I wasn't trying to hurt him, right?

I continued to weigh the pros and cons of dating Jackson long into the night. Were my obstacles really worth not giving us a shot?

In the end, I decided I didn't think they were.

CHAPTER THIRTEEN

PRESTON and I were driving to school when Coach Scruggs finally sent the email out with the team roster. It had been several days since tryouts, and we'd all been waiting not-so-patiently for the players to be announced. Every day, Daria and I would ask the other if they'd heard anything yet. And every day, we both had to say no.

So, I was thankful that Preston was driving when my phone dinged with that long-awaited email. That meant I was free to read the list right away. I quickly scanned to see my name listed on the varsity team, with the word "co-captain" next to it. A few lines beneath that was Daria's name.

I did a little victory dance in the passenger seat.

Preston jerked his head in my direction. "Good news?"

"Coach Scruggs finally sent out the roster."

"She really was drawing it out, wasn't she?"

I nodded, thinking about how jealous I'd been when the boys' coach emailed the team roster the same night. But finally, I was vindicated. I'd made varsity, even while on athletic probation.

I'm co-captain of the girls' team!" I squealed.

"That's great."

I shot off two quick texts. The first one was to Daria.

Charlie: Congrats!!!! Looks like we really are stuck together now. Can't wait to boss you around.
Daria: You're never gonna get rid of me, even if we go in opposite directions after graduation. Just you wait and see!

The second one was to Jackson.

Charlie: I made varsity and co-captain. I'm SO excited!
Romeo: That's great, babe.

My breath caught in my chest. I hadn't told him that I was willing to date him yet, but I still liked the way that word looked on the screen of my phone.

Charlie: Babe?
Romeo: Just trying it out.
Charlie: Uh, huh. Better be careful calling me that.
Romeo: You know I'm a rebel. It's why I get to see you at Helping Hands on Saturday.
Charlie: Whatever. We both know you're a softie.

He sent a string of emojis—an angry face, a middle finger...a weird mask guy? I didn't know the meaning behind half the little cartoons on the emoji keyboard, but I could tell this was his "I'm not a sweet guy" argument. Little did he know, I wanted a sweet guy.

I wanted him.

"Wow. Who knew you were so excited about the team?" Preston said, causing me to look up quickly. "I mean, you already knew you were going to make it, right?"

"Yeah. I guess everything with athletic probation had me on edge. It's good to know that's one hurdle I don't have to worry about."

I hadn't meant to say that last part out loud. If Preston asked me about my other hurdles, I wasn't sure how I'd tell him it was Brooks. Thankfully, my brother was off in basketball la-la land.

"This is going to be the best year ever, Charlie. We're both seniors about to graduate. We'll both be on varsity when the scouts come this year. Hopefully, we'll get scholarships and go to college without massive loans. It's gonna be great!"

And those things were great. I just hoped everything else could somehow fall into place.

WHEN I BUMPED into Daria later that day, she looked like she'd seen a ghost.

"Daria, are you—"

She put up a hand to stop me. "We need to talk. Now. Let's sneak out to the football field for lunch."

"I can't," I argued. "If Mr. Richards catches me, I'll be in a lot of trouble."

My best friend held up her phone. On the screen was the infamous picture Anderson had sent to me. I put my hand over the screen and looked around quickly, making sure no one saw it.

Daria lifted her eyebrows. "Come to the football field. Now."

She started walking down the hall, away from the cafeteria without looking back to make sure I was behind her. I scanned the hallways for any signs of Rosemark administration before following her out the double doors, and out to the field.

Neither one of us spoke, and my mind raced the entire walk out. Who had sent that to Daria? There was only one person I knew who had that picture. Anderson. But now I worried that he'd shared it with more people than Daria and me. How many people knew my secret?

And what did Daria think of me now? I'd been keeping this from her, and she found out from my sleazy ex-boyfriend. She had to be angry at me, but I wasn't sure how bad it was.

Like, you took a fry without permission angry?

Or, we're never hanging out again angry?

My stomach twisted as I played out the different possible scenarios in my head until we were standing beneath the bleachers.

Daria turned to face me. She jerked her hands upward. "How could you?"

My words rushed out in a jumble. "I'm sorry. I didn't mean for this to happen. We were working at Helping Hands together, and he was so sweet. I really liked talking to him. And then he took me to the maze and drove me home the other day when you were at the dentist."

I stopped and took a deep breath. "I'm sorry, Daria. I don't know what to say."

Daria closed her eyes. "You think I'm mad that you like Brooks?" she asked slowly.

"Uh, yeah?"

"Then you really are an idiot." She shook her head and opened her eyes. "That's not why I'm mad. I mean, I think it's incredibly stupid considering the Senior Year Rematch and rivalry with your brother. But that's not why I'm upset with you."

"It's not?" I was so confused.

"How long have we been friends?"

"Since fifth grade," I answered.

"And are we best friends?"

I nodded, still not sure where she was going with all this.

"Then I shouldn't be finding out about who you have a crush on from Anderson! He sent that picture to me earlier with some text about me helping get you two back together. Said if I didn't, he was going to make sure Preston saw it."

My eyes went wide.

"Of course, you'd already told me about the corn maze, and I thought it was just some random dude. So, I told him to go ahead and send it."

I gasped. "Oh, no!"

I was ready to run back to the school to find Preston. I was prepared to run away from the school and never look back.

"Don't worry, he didn't. Anderson explained why that picture was so important. And why I should help him."

I rubbed a hand over my face. This was bad. This was so, so bad. "What did you tell him?"

"I told him not to stop me when I dragged you outside during lunch. I told him not to do anything hasty because I am your friend, Charlie Royce. I've got your back. On the court, off the court. Always. But I can't do that if you keep secrets from me."

Too embarrassed to look my best friend in the eye, my gaze went to my feet. I'd been keeping secrets, and she was mad because it meant she couldn't look out for me.

I didn't deserve her.

"Listen, I understand why you didn't tell me. Your brother really has it out for Brooks, but I'm not him. I don't care who you date, as long as they're a decent human being. So, I need you to tell me, is Brooks a good guy or some jerk like Anderson?"

"He's a good guy. And his name is Jackson."

"Jackson is a much better name than Brooks."

I smiled. "It is. Jackson really is great. And honestly, I'm relieved you finally know. I hated keeping him a secret from you. Especially, since I was about to tell him I would be his girlfriend."

"Oh, wow." Daria took a deep breath. "Then we need to decide what to do about Anderson because that dude is crazy with a capital C."

I thought about the way he'd acted these last couple of weeks and couldn't agree more. "What I don't get is, why does he care? Anderson is the one who cheated on me. He's the one who seemed thrilled about breaking up."

"And boys are like toddlers. They might not want to play with a toy, but that doesn't mean he wants anyone else playing with it."

I laughed. "What am I? A bicycle?"

Daria choked on a laugh, and her eyes went wide. "Do me a favor, and don't carry that analogy out too far. I think you'll really regret not picking a kickball or blocks or anything else if you do."

I thought about what she meant by that. There was nothing wrong with a bicycle. You rode them and...

Right. Anderson was a jerk and would take that and make it into something perverted.

"You thought too hard," Daria said in response to the face I was making.

I nodded.

"Fine. Let's think about it this way instead. I'm sure Anderson saw you with Brooks, and it probably made him realize what a terrible guy he is. And he's going to take it out on you."

"Ugh. So, what do we do?"

"Have you considered going to Preston, and just telling him about Brooks?"

I shook my head. "I love my brother, but he would not take it well. It's like he thinks Jackson Brooks has it out for him."

"And does he?"

"I don't know." I shrugged. "We don't really talk about it. It's easier that way."

Daria shook her head. "Girl. You are digging yourself a hole here."

"I know."

And the thing was, I really did know. I was avoiding my brother when I was with Jackson. And I was keeping the guy I liked from Preston. I was compartmentalizing my life, hoping the two circles would never meet. But they would meet. And soon.

Basketball season was right around the corner, and the game against Pinebrook was the guys' season opener. There would be so much pressure on both sides to win, and I wasn't sure who I would cheer for. A win for either team would mean upset for someone I cared about.

This whole thing was a mess.

The desire to run returned. I could take a vacation, just until basketball season was over. Sure, I'd miss the opportunity to get an athletic scholarship. But who needed college?

My thoughts continued to cycle through one irrational thought after another until I looked back up at Daria. She watched me with kind eyes.

"I don't know what to do," I said.

"Girl. Me neither, but we'll figure it out together."

CHAPTER FOURTEEN

DARIA and I hadn't figured anything out. We'd been texting ideas back and forth but always came up short.

I considered telling Preston the truth. I knew he and Jackson had a grudge, but maybe they could be civil to one another off the court. Yes, it was unlikely, but it was so much better than the other option. I'd just decided I was ready to date Jackson. I didn't want it to end before we had a chance to explore it further.

I wasn't willing to settle for either option, which meant I had no plan when Anderson pulled me aside during lunch on Friday.

"Take a walk with me," he said, linking his arm in mine. He pulled me toward the football field. I knew we were going to the bleachers and, if I had any say, I'd never go under there again for as long as I lived.

Nothing good ever came of it.

I didn't think Anderson would physically hurt me, but I didn't want to hear what he had to say.

"I know about you and Brooks, Charlie. You know that. Daria knows that. I kinda thought you'd come talk to me by now."

I shook my head. "I don't know what you want from me, Anderson. You are the one who cheated on me. You are the one who went out with Linzie. Why do you want me to be your girlfriend so badly?"

His laugh was cruel. "Really, Charlie? You think I want to get back with you?"

I was confused. "Uh, yeah? That's what you told Daria. Why else would you be blackmailing me?"

"You keyed my car, Charlie. I had to drive around for a week with that on my door. Everywhere I went, people gave me dirty looks. Linzie felt uncomfortable riding with me. And my parents were pissed. They said I'd embarrassed them—ruined the Webb name."

"I don't understand."

"I want to see you suffer the way I suffered. Either you break up with Brooks and pretend to date me, or I tell Preston all about your night at the corn maze."

It didn't make sense. Anderson had been parading Linzie all over school ever since our breakup. I imagined she'd be pretty mad if she saw the two of us together. Unless...

"Did Linzie dump you?"

His cool facade broke for a split second. "It doesn't matter."

Translation: Yes, she did.

"Back to the matter at hand." He smiled, but there was no warmth in it. "That picture I sent you isn't the only one I have of you and Brooks."

Goosebumps broke out up and down my arms. "Wait. Have you been stalking me?"

He laughed. "I haven't had to. You've been flaunting it like you want to get caught. I can't wait to see your brother's face when I tell him. You think you know how much he hates Brooks? You have no idea. You should hear the way he talks about him when you're not around."

"Don't tell him," I said, hating how it sounded like I was begging. Who was I kidding? Anderson had me freaked out. Of course, I was begging.

"Come to Sammi's Halloween party with me on Saturday night. Wear something sexy and pretend like you're falling all over me."

"Oh, yeah, because that'll be believable. Charlie Royce dressed in something skimpy for Halloween."

Anderson shrugged. "Maybe it'll just show how determined you are to get back with me."

I pressed my lips together.

"You make a big show of you crawling back to me, and we'll be even."

"Just like that?"

Anderson grinned. "Just like that."

My eyes narrowed in suspicion. Playing his girlfriend in front of everyone would make for a miserable night, but it still seemed too easy. I knew I was missing something. I just didn't know what.

I thought of Preston, and how he might react. I may have thought I was willing to risk it all to date Jackson in the safety of my room, but when faced with the reality of having to make a choice, I realized I didn't have a choice.

I nodded. "Fine. I'll do it."

I waited for Anderson to walk back to the school building. I still had a few minutes until the bell rang. And, of course, that was when Jackson decided to text me. Instead of feeling the usual rush of butterflies at seeing his name on my screen, a rock had taken their fluttery place. I'd made a deal with the devil, and now I had to live with it.

11:56 AM
Romeo: Hey! What are you doing tomorrow night? My cousin is having this thing, and I thought maybe we could go together. I know you aren't ready for another date, but there'll be lots of people there, so it doesn't really count. Just an excuse to spend more time together. What do you think???

I would have loved to say yes, but I'd just committed to going to the Halloween party with Anderson. Maybe it was better this way—to say no right away, instead of having to break plans with him.

Charlie: Sorry! I can't. I already made other plans.
Romeo: Bummer. I guess that's what I get for waiting. At

least I get to see your beautiful face tomorrow at the soup kitchen.

He put a couple of heart-eyed emojis after the word kitchen. A sad smile touched my lips. I had no idea how I was going to face Jackson in the morning. How could I look him in the eyes knowing I was about to throw myself at Anderson?

Not to mention the game between Rosemark and Pinebrook was right around the corner. It was stupid to think I could have a happily ever after with Jackson. We'd always end in tragedy.

I should have known with a code name like Romeo, we were doomed from the start.

I couldn't see him anymore. That was the only possible way to avoid breaking both of our hearts. Better to end things *before* they got any more serious, right? Jackson was so clearly into me, which was adorable and romantic and everything I didn't know I wanted.

But Preston was my brother. We'd been through a lot together, and we always had each other's backs. I couldn't keep seeing Jackson behind his back no matter how much I wanted to, especially now that Anderson was blackmailing me.

My fingers trembled as I typed my reply.

Charlie: Were you serious when you said you would stop going to Helping Hands until I finished my commitment?

I hit send before I could change my mind.

Romeo: Why are you asking me that? I thought we were going to give "us" a shot first?
Charlie: Will you or won't you stay home tomorrow?

It was a long time before he responded. The bell had already rung in the distance, but I refused to move from this spot until he answered my question.

Romeo: I'll stay home until December. That way you won't have to worry about seeing me ever again.

I could almost hear the frustration in his voice when I read the words on the screen. My fingers hovered over the keyboard. I wanted to tell him everything, but I couldn't. He'd want to fix it, or he wouldn't understand why this was such a hard decision for me.

I settled on two words: I'm sorry.

But in the end, I deleted them before ever hitting send.

CHAPTER FIFTEEN

TRUE TO HIS WORD, Jackson didn't show up for Helping Hands the following day. But that didn't mean I hadn't felt his presence the entire time I'd volunteered at the soup kitchen.

From Mila's curious gazes to Mrs. Gibbs dirty looks, it was obvious where everyone placed the blame for Jackson's absence.

When I'd finished my time giving food to the less fortunate, I raced to the local thrift shop. Anderson hadn't given me much time to come up with something to wear to Sammi's party, and my parents weren't going to dish out the money for their little girl to go buy something that showed off way too much skin. So, I was stuck doing the best I could with my limited savings from my summer job.

I had scoured the racks looking for something that fit me, could double as a Halloween costume, and didn't smell like grandma's attic. It wasn't nearly as easy as I'd hoped it would be, but an hour later, I settled on a combination of items I hoped would satisfy Anderson—plaid skirt I could roll up until it was too short, knee-high socks, and a button-down shirt that I'd tie just above my navel. I planned to top my ensemble off with braided pigtails.

I didn't want to see my parents or Preston's disap-proving looks, so when I got dressed in my room, I made sure my skirt was two inches above my knees, and the shirt was buttoned all the way down and covered my stomach completely.

Once I was as satisfied as I could be with my appear-ance, I met my brother out in the hall. He wore a basketball jersey and an inflatable doughnut around his waist.

"What are you supposed to be?" I asked as he beamed down at me.

Preston lifted his hands like he was poised to shoot a basketball. "Dunkin' Doughnut, duh."

I shook my head. "I should have known you'd do some-thing cheesy."

"Wait until you see Beth. She's going to be Starbucks, and we're going to fight all night over who makes the best coffee."

I tried to smile but couldn't quite get there after every-thing that had happened the previous week—and knowing what was still to come.

"And look at you in a dress," Pres continued. "What exactly are you supposed to be, Charlie?"

"Catholic schoolgirl? I don't know! I didn't have a lot of time to pull something together."

"Well, maybe if you didn't wait until the day before the party to decide you were going to come, you would have found something a little better than your sad, conservative Britney Spears costume." Preston waved a hand at my clothing.

"We can't all be as clever as you, can we?"

"I wouldn't even try," he joked as we walked down the hall and said goodbye to our parents.

They made a big fuss over Preston's costume and were mostly baffled by my choice. I used the same last-minute argument with them, and thankfully they both just shrugged it off.

Don't worry guys, I thought. It's about to get way worse. I was just happy they wouldn't be able to see any of it.

We were told to be home by midnight just as we walked out the front door. Preston agreed to drive to Sammi's, and I texted Anderson to let him know we were on our way.

9:30 PM
Charlie: We'll be there soon.
Anderson: What are you wearing?

Ew. Could he be any creepier? With every passing day after our break-up, I saw him more clearly. I couldn't believe I'd ever been attracted to him. I sighed and played my part.

Charlie: Naughty school girl.

Anderson: Niiiiiice. Now, don't forget. You're coming tonight to beg me to get back together. I want you all over me. If not, I'm showing Pres the picture in front of everyone.

Bile rose in the back of my throat.

Charlie: Can't wait.

I continued to stare down at my phone. I hated this stupid situation so much. I'd all but broken up with Jackson, and I was still stuck following Anderson's every command.

"Everything okay?" Preston managed to sneak a glance in my direction and looked down at my phone.

I shut off the screen, even though I knew he wouldn't have been able to read it in that short amount of time. "Uh, yeah. Just..."

I paused. While I didn't want him to think I was in trouble, I also didn't want him to be ashamed of my behavior that evening.

"Just a little tired," I said hoping he would drop it.

"You sure?"

I forced a smile. "I'm sure everything will be much better once we get to Sammi's."

. . .

EVERYTHING WAS NOT BETTER ONCE we got there.

I'd quickly run to the bathroom once we walked into Sammi's mansion of a house. I hiked up my skirt and tied off my shirt, feeling very much like the village prostitute. It was one thing to dress this way because I wanted to. It was a completely different thing knowing it was to keep my ex-boyfriend happy.

I tried to ignore the strange looks I got walking around the first floor of the house and resisted the urge to tug on the skirt so that it was covering more skin. Careful not to bump into Daria or Preston, I walked room to room until I found Anderson. He was with some of the other basketball players—not anyone Pres or I really hung out with. He wore a cop uniform, complete with handcuffs hanging from his hip.

He didn't see me right away, so I stood next to him, a frown on my face, waiting for him to acknowledge my presence. When he turned and saw me standing there, his expression turned predatory—from the gleam in his slightly narrowed eyes, to the way his lips curled in a smile that was anything but kind.

Anderson leaned in and whispered in my ear. "Remember, you're supposed to be madly in love with me. So, turn that frown upside down."

When he stepped back, he winked at me. I reluctantly lifted the corners of my mouth into a tight-lipped smile.

"Charlie!" Anderson said loud enough to gain the

attention of some nearby people. "What are you saying? You want to get back together with me?"

He lifted his brows, ever so slightly, telling me to get started.

I took a deep breath and stepped closer. I answered just loud enough to make sure those closest to us would hear. "I miss you so much, Anderson." My left hand trembled as it found the button-front of his shirt.

I put my other palm flat against his chest, not sure if I was surprised or not when I realized his heartbeat was steady beneath it. Anderson wasn't affected by me, whatsoever. He'd been serious when he said this was all for payback.

"I don't know," he pondered loudly. "You said and did some pretty mean things. How do I know you're serious?"

I barely contained my sigh, and only after I bit the inside of my cheek. "Please, Anderson. Take me back?"

He chuckled and looked over to the guys who were with him that night. One looked as amused as I imagined Anderson felt, but the others seemed more confused. I guessed it had a lot to do with the fact I was Preston's sister and all the drama that had played out a few weeks earlier.

"Come on, Charlie." Anderson wrapped his arm around my shoulders. "Let's go get something to drink."

I walked alongside Anderson, mostly keeping my eyes on him. As much as he disgusted me, it was easier to swallow than the looks my fellow classmates gave me. Even Sammi looked weirded out by how cozy my ex-boyfriend and I were acting.

At least I could find comfort knowing Jackson was at his cousin's and wouldn't see me like this.

My phone buzzed in the small pocket of my skirt. I managed to pull it out while Anderson was talking to some people.

10:03 PM
Daria: What the heck is going on????? Tell me you did NOT get back with Anderson. Tell me this is some kind of joke.

I didn't know what to tell her, so I stuck my phone back in my pocket. When it vibrated again, I ignored it. It didn't matter how many question marks Daria put at the end of her texts, there was no making sense of this situation.

I allowed Anderson to take me room by room throughout the house. I knew his goal was to make sure as many people as possible saw us together. He wanted everyone to see how I was dressed, and how I was all over him.

I hated every minute of it.

When we found a quiet room, I jerked away from Anderson's possessive touch. "Are we done?"

"Almost."

His eyes went to something behind me. I started to turn and see what it was, but Anderson leaned in close and ran his hand over my cheek. "Let's go out back for a little while," he said a little too loudly.

I thought of the low temperature and my general lack of clothing. "But it's cold outside."

"Don't worry, I'll keep you warm." Again, his voice boomed in the small, quiet space we stood.

I let out a resigned sigh and let Anderson wrap his arm around me once more. He led me to the room's exit, and I finally saw what, or more accurately who, he had looked at earlier.

It wasn't some random person walking by the room, as I had hoped.

It wasn't even Preston or Daria standing there.

No, it was Jackson with a hurt-filled expression. I felt the knife in my heart twist a little more as he turned and walked away, knowing I'd just sealed our fate.

CHAPTER SIXTEEN

APPARENTLY, the near-freezing night air was too much for Anderson, because we were outside all of ten minutes before he was ushering me back inside. But that didn't mean the night was over.

No, now we had gossip fodder as he paraded me all over the house.

We hadn't been back inside for very long when Preston came storming over, looking menacing despite the pool floaty that was still around his waist. Beth stood off in the distance dressed like a drink from Starbucks.

"What the hell is going on?" Pres yelled drawing my attention from his girlfriend.

His eyes were narrowed, his skin flushed in anger. "Why are you harassing my sister, Anderson? I thought you learned your lesson last time you messed with her."

Anderson smirked at my brother but didn't say anything. It only served to infuriate Preston more.

"I'm serious, Anderson. I don't care if you're a great point guard. You're not going to treat her like this."

We were starting to gather a crowd. Anderson looked down at me expectantly. That was my cue.

"Actually, Pres, I'm the one who sought out Anderson." I cleared my throat. "I'm hoping to get back together with him."

"You what?" His eyes were wide, and he turned back to Beth as if looking for some kind of confirmation. She lifted her hands letting him know she was just as lost as he was. "I don't understand."

I closed my eyes and took a deep breath. "I realized I was overreacting about everything. He *is* the hottest guy in school, and I came here hoping he'd take me back."

Preston ran his hand through his hair. "And that's why you changed your mind so last minute about the party?"

I lifted my shoulders. "I figured he would be here and thought it was a great chance to get his attention."

Anderson finally spoke up. "Did you see what she's wearing? Of course, she got my attention."

"I'm going to kill you!"

Preston shot forward toward Anderson, but not before I could step between them. I stuck my hands out and pushed them against his chest. I could hear the excited chatter around us and saw a couple of phones in my peripheral. This was going to be all over Rosemark before school on Monday, but I couldn't think about that right now.

"Stop it!" I yelled at my brother over the sounds of the party.

"What does he have on you?"

"Nothing," I answered quickly. My eyes darted back and forth. "Why would you think that?"

"Because I know how you feel about Anderson. Something isn't right here."

"You know what?" Anderson interrupted again, leaning around me. "You're right. Something isn't right. I thought I might take Charlie back tonight, but now I can see how she reeks of desperation. Sorry, babe, but it's not a good look for you."

My cheeks felt like they were on fire.

"I mean, you think you can dress like that, and I'll want to be your boyfriend. You really are crazy, Charlie Royce."

I shook my head. I finally saw the final puzzle piece. It wasn't enough to parade me all over tonight. Anderson had wanted the opportunity to tear me down in front of everyone. He was an even bigger jerk than I thought.

I felt the sting of tears in my eyes, and no matter how much I fought, they started falling down my cheeks.

Anderson had already walked off, and I could hear little snippets of what he said to anyone who would listen. Something about me being pathetic, sad, and crazy. I honestly couldn't determine which words were his, and those that came from other people.

A couple of people still had their phones aimed in my direction, so I flipped them off.

"Charlie." Preston put his hand on my shoulder.

I jerked away. "Not now, Pres."

The patio still looked relatively empty, and I felt so numb, I doubted the cold would be nearly as unbearable as earlier. I stormed out the French doors and found a spot far from the gazes of my classmates.

The braids were the first thing to go. I threw the hair ties on the wooden deck. My fingers combed through the kinks in my hair. When I was satisfied, I untied my shirt and buttoned the rest of the buttons. I unrolled the waist of my skirt until it covered the tops of my thighs, and sat down, pulling my knees to my chest.

And there, in the cold Colorado air, I let the tears come in hot rivers down my cheeks.

I cried because Anderson had humiliated me in front of everyone I knew. I cried because of the secrets I kept from Preston, who only wanted to protect me. I cried because I was still on athletic probation and I was worried I might miss out on my chance at a college scholarship from basketball.

But I also cried for Jackson. I'd fallen hard for him in these last few weeks. If it hadn't been for Anderson's stupid picture, I wouldn't have told him not to go to Helping Hands. We wouldn't have broken up—if that's what you could call what happened—and he wouldn't have seen Anderson and me all over each other.

I only hoped he wasn't there when Anderson had dealt the finishing blow.

Who was I kidding? He didn't have to be at the live

event. There were going to be plenty of videos floating around.

And why had he been here anyway? Wasn't he supposed to be at his cousin's house?

When my phone buzzed for the hundredth time, I pulled it out of my pocket.

10:42 PM

Daria: Where are you???? Are you okay?? I was in the bathroom and came out and Veronica told me what happened.

Daria: I don't see Preston or Anderson anywhere. I hope they're not fighting.

I was about to put my phone away when another text came through.

Daria: What happened to no more secrets?

Charlie: You're right. Here ya go: Anderson played me like a fool. He got his revenge. Hopefully, it's over.

Daria: Wow.

Charlie: Oh, yeah... That's not all. Jackson was here tonight. He saw Anderson and me together.

Daria: Whaaaat???

Charlie: I'm on the back porch freezing my butt off. I'll be inside in a few.

Daria: Are you sure you're OK??

Charlie: No more secrets. I promise. I just need one more minute.

Daria: Fine. But if you're not back inside by 11, I'm sending the search party.

Charlie: Please do! If I'm not back inside, I'm probably a popsicle.

I saw that I had a few more texts from people wanting to know what happened with Anderson. There was something special about drama that brought everyone out from the wood-work. These were people I didn't talk to on a daily, or even weekly, basis. Why did they think they had special privileges?

I deleted them all until I was left with a lone text from Anderson sent just minutes before the one from Daria.

10:39 PM

Anderson: Great job in there. Those tears were almost believable. Too bad I know you don't have a heart in that perfectly formed chest of yours.

Charlie: Are we done?

Anderson: For now.

Charlie: You can't blackmail me forever!

Anderson: I guess we'll see, won't we?

A chill came over me, which was caused not only by the icy breeze that had started but also from the promise of more torture.

I reconsidered telling Preston everything but seeing the murder in his expression tonight gave me pause. There was only one other time I'd seen that look on his face, and it was after Jackson Brooks had made him miss the winning shot for Rosemark. That game had cost them the finals.

There was no way Preston would just "get over" his sister dating his rival—not that I was in any danger of that after Jackson had seen me with Anderson. But even if I never saw Jackson again, Preston's grudge would only grow if he saw those pictures.

I didn't want to think about what would happen to either Preston or Jackson with that kind of tension on the court.

When I didn't think I could survive the cold any longer, I decided it was time to go inside and find Daria. But when I stood up and turned around, I came face to face with the boy of my musings.

Jackson stood in front of me wearing his Pinebrook letterman jacket and jeans. I hadn't gotten a good look at him earlier, and I wasn't sure if he wore some kind of costume under his jacket. Not that it mattered. Jackson was here, and in his hands were a bright pink puffer coat that looked vaguely familiar and a thick, wool blanket.

"I'm sure you have a vendetta against pink, but it was all I could find in my cousin's closet."

I finally connected the dots. "Your cousin is Sammi."

He nodded.

"And this Halloween party was her thing you invited me to."

Another bob of his head before he held out the jacket. "Put the jacket on, Charlie."

I stared at it for a few seconds before finally taking it from Jackson. It was doubtful Sammi knew he had it. I wondered what she would think of Charlie Royce wearing her clothing. I imagined she'd be having a fit for more than one reason.

My arms pushed through the sleeves, but it wasn't easy. While we were both thin, Sammi was at least one size smaller than me. With some effort, I eventually wrangled it on.

My entire body shook as I crossed my arms over my chest to warm myself. I hadn't realized just how cold I was until I'd gotten a taste of heat. I looked back up at Jackson. "What are you doing out here?"

"I needed to talk to you." He waved to where I'd just been sitting. "Can we sit for a minute?"

I lowered my chin to my chest. "Okay."

The two of us sat side-by-side, and once we were situated, Jackson put the blanket over our legs. "Is this warm enough? Would you rather go inside?"

Tears started forming again as I shook my head.

I couldn't understand why he was being so nice to me. Part of me wished he wasn't. It would be a lot easier to forget about him if he wasn't currently fussing over the blanket, making sure every inch of skin was protected from the cold.

I kept my gaze trained in front of me. "What do you want, Jackson?"

"I don't know where to start. I keep trying to figure out if I want to yell at you or beg you to talk to me. I don't know if I should be mad at you for what happened in there or sad."

I felt my frustration returning. Jackson had done nothing wrong, but I snapped at him anyway. "We were never dating, so you don't have to feel guilty for not wanting to be with me, okay? Just let it go."

"I heard your ex joking in the kitchen. He didn't know I was standing there."

I turned to face him. "What did he say?"

I hated how eager my voice was, but I needed to know what he was saying to people when I wasn't there.

"He talked about some picture, and how easy it was to manipulate you." Jackson closed his eyes. "They were all laughing at you, and it made me crazy. It took everything in me not to lay into him in the middle of my aunt and uncle's kitchen."

It looked like Anderson wasn't keeping his end of the bargain in our little arrangement. I let out a sigh.

"What does this dude have on you?" Jackson asked.

"A picture of us from the night we went to the corn maze together. He threatened to tell my brother if I didn't come to this party and act like I was in love with him."

Jackson cussed under his breath. "Charlie, I know Royce and I are competitive on the court, but is all this really worth it? That guy made a fool of you in there."

I took a deep breath, knowing I was about to break some sort of sibling code. "Preston skipped school a couple of weeks ago to get a private basketball lesson because he heard you had extra training all summer."

Jackson made a "hmm" sound in the back of his throat.

"Yeah, and he and the rest of the team even have a special name for their game against you. The Senior Year Rematch. It's a big deal for the entire team, but especially Preston."

"So, what does this mean for us?"

I shrugged. "I think we need to end this before it gets any worse. It was silly to think we could have anything serious."

When I started to turn my face away, Jackson lifted his hand to stop me. His fingers were cold, yet gentle, against my skin. "Do you want to end things?"

Unable to speak from the intensity of Jackson's gaze, I shook my head in response.

"I don't either. What if we kept it a secret?"

I snorted. "No one wants to be in a secret relationship. That's a major red flag. Either somebody is embarrassed or already in a relationship."

"But we know that's not the case. And it wouldn't be forever. Just until the end of basketball season."

He made it sound so simple. "What if Rosemark loses to Pinebrook again this year? Do you think Preston is just going to give up?"

Jackson shrugged. "I don't know, Charlie. I'm trying here because I like you. A lot. And I want to find a way to make us happen. But if you really don't want to date me, tell me now, and I will leave you alone."

"Jackson."

"Do you want me to leave you alone?"

I shook my head. "No."

"Then we'll figure this out."

"Okay," I whispered in the stillness of the night.

Jackson leaned closer, and I subconsciously licked my lips. His eyes went straight to my mouth like an arrow to a bullseye. That small shift in his gaze caused my heart to leap in my chest.

"So, does this mean we're officially dating?" he asked.

"I mean, as long as you consider a secret relationship we can't tell anyone about dating, then sure, we're dating."

I giggled, but Jackson's face was serious.

"Good, because I've been kicking myself for making that stupid rule about no kissing until we're official."

Oh.

Jackson took a shaky breath, and I realized my own had started coming more quickly. He brushed some hair, whether real or imaginary, away from my face and let his hands linger on my cheek.

And before I knew it, his mouth pressed against mine. The kiss was tentative at first but quickly turned urgent. My hands wrapped around the back of his head, and my fingers played with his hair. Jackson kept one hand on my face, while the other ran up and down my arm. Even through the puffy jacket, his touch warmed me.

Our lips tangled up in one another until I heard the sound of the door slamming.

Jackson and I broke apart and looked toward the house.

Preston stood there. I'd thought he had looked angry inside when he was yelling at Anderson, but that seemed playful compared to the way he looked now.

A vein throbbed in his forehead, his eyes were narrowed slits, and a sneer overtook his mouth. "Get away from my sister!" he growled through clenched teeth.

Jackson stood up, took a few steps away from me, and put his hands in the air. "I don't want any trouble."

I jumped up and took a couple of steps toward my brother. "Pres."

He shook his head at me and I stopped. The three of us stood there in tense silence until the door opened, and a couple of people poured out—including Anderson. The look on his face was pure glee.

Preston started cussing Jackson out. All the while, Jackson stayed silent.

"Preston, stop!" I finally yelled after the verbal attacks became too much to listen to.

"This is why you've been acting so weird, isn't it?" he spat. "How long have you been hooking up with the enemy behind my back, *Charlotte?*"

I recoiled slightly at the use of my given name. I couldn't remember the last time he'd used it and knew he must be blind with rage to say it now. "I haven't been..." I started, considering Jackson and I hadn't been technically dating until that night. I turned to Jackson and saw the flash of hurt across his features. "What I mean is..."

Tears fell down my cheeks, and I was unable to say

anything. Not that there was anything I could say to make things better. My eyes went from person to person.

Preston looked at me with anger. There was no doubt he felt betrayed by finding me making out with his biggest rival.

Jackson watched me with hurt in his eyes for the second time that evening. He'd done nothing but put himself out there time and time again, only to have me act wishy-washy about our relationship.

Anderson's face looked like it would split if his smile got any bigger. He was having a field day watching this play out. Not only had he gotten to embarrass me in front of everyone, but he also got to watch the moment when Preston found out my secret anyway.

I felt overwhelmed by so many emotions as everyone stood watching me. They were all waiting for me to say or do something, so I did the only thing I could think of.

I turned and ran.

CHAPTER SEVENTEEN

THANK goodness I still had Sammi's pink jacket.

I'd left the scene at her house in such a hurry, I hadn't really thought anything through. I ran for about a mile down the long road that led to her house. But once the cold air became too much pushing in and out of my lungs, I stopped.

It was then that the weight of everything began to sink in.

It was nearly midnight, I was walking through an area that was not densely populated, and it was near freezing.

I pulled the jacket tightly around my torso, and I continued to walk toward my house. It was several miles away, and I'd never make curfew. But I didn't know who to ask for help.

Several cars drove by me as I did my dramatic walk of shame on the side of the road. Some would honk, some would holler, but not a single person stopped to see if I was okay.

And I was so not okay.

I continued for several more minutes before my entire body shook. This wasn't going to work. I needed to have someone come get me.

When I spotted a tree stump a short distance from the street, I walked over and sat down. I pulled out my phone and called my dad. It didn't even finish the first ring when he answered.

"Charlie? Where are you? Are you okay?" His voice was full of panic.

"Dad, I need you to—" My voice broke off into violent sobbing. But I eventually managed to get out enough words to ask him to come get me.

I heard the jingle of keys through the speaker. "I'm on my way."

We stayed on the phone, not exactly talking, but more of my dad reassuring me he was on his way, and me telling him where I was once I was able to speak.

My phone buzzed, and I pulled it away from my face. There was a message from Daria on the screen.

11:30 PM
Daria: WHERE ARE YOU????? I've been looking for you everywhere. I lost you in the crowd. Veronica said you ran away from the party! Tell me you're not dead in a ditch.

I put my dad on speaker—who was still talking to me like a spooked animal—so I could text my best friend.

Charlie: I'm on the side of the road.
Daria: WHERE??? Put on Find My Friends and I'll come get you!!
Charlie: My dad is already on his way. I'm going to be in so much trouble, but I didn't know what to do. Pres found out about Jackson.
Daria: Girl, I am so sorry.

"Okay, Charlie-bear, I'm heading down Oak right now. Where are you?"

I switched the speaker back to normal and held the phone to my ear. "I'm going to stand near the edge of the road. I'm wearing a pink jacket."

He made a coughing sound. "Pink?"

"Yeah, pink." I saw headlights nearing, and I waved my hand. "Is that you?"

"Yep. I'll see you in a sec."

We hung up, and I stepped aside as my dad pulled over onto the shoulder. I wasted no time getting into his SUV. "Thanks, Dad," I said without looking in his direction.

He made a U-turn and started driving to our house. "Where's Preston? I cannot believe he'd just leave you at a party. When he gets home—"

"He didn't leave me," I interrupted. "I ran away from the party."

"You what?" My dad's fingers tightened on the steering wheel. "Do you have any idea what could have happened to you out here? What if you were hit by a car, or someone drove by and snatched you up?"

My dad's voice cracked, and he cleared his throat. After checking his mirrors, he pulled back over to the side of the road, put the car in park, and turned to look at me. "After your mom died, I was afraid I would fall apart. I loved her so much. But then I realized I had this little girl who needed me to be strong and take care of her. And so I was."

"I always assumed it would be you and me against the world. But then I met Kathy, and I discovered I was able to love again. I love her and Preston very much, you know that, right?"

I nodded, unsure of where he was going with this.

"I love them, but you are still my little girl. Charlie, if anything ever happened to you, I don't know what I would do. It would break me."

"I'm sorry, Dad. I wasn't thinking. Everything happened so fast."

I relayed what had happened to him, conveniently leaving out the part where Jackson and I were making out when Preston found us. When I was done, my dad pulled back onto the road and started driving back toward the house.

He didn't say anything else, and I didn't either. The silence in the car was unbearable. I couldn't decide if my dad was angry, disappointed, or something else. I hated not knowing where I stood with him.

The traffic was light, and it didn't take long until we got home. I opened the car door, and raced to the front door, looking forward to being alone in my room.

"Wait," my dad called. "I want you to go to the living room and wait for me."

He pulled out his phone, hit a couple buttons on the screen, and lifted it to his ear. I lingered at the front door of our house and listened.

"Preston, I need you to come home right now. No stops, do you understand?" He paused, his face contorted slightly as he listened to the voice on the other end. "I don't care, you have ten minutes."

When Dad hung up, his gaze zeroed in on where I stood eavesdropping.

"Inside, Charlie," he said, his voice firm.

My dad didn't have to tell me twice, and he followed right behind me as we walked into the house. When I turned toward the living room, he went down the hall to his bedroom. And even though he shut the door, I could hear his and Mom's voices speaking in hushed tones.

I sat down on the couch, and as my body adjusted to the warmer temperature inside, I finally shed the pink jacket I'd inadvertently stolen from Sammi. I'd have to return it to her somehow, though I had no desire to talk to her or anyone at Rosemark after that party.

The idea of getting expelled and going to the Hope for

the Future Academy for the rest of the year was looking a lot more appealing than it was a few weeks ago.

I groaned and slumped against the back of the couch. I covered my eyes with my hands as the murmuring voices continued in the other room. I couldn't make out the words they spoke—wasn't sure I wanted to.

The sound of the front door had me jerking up. Preston loomed in the doorway. The donut from his costume was gone, and he just wore his basketball shirt and pants. That and a massive black eye.

"Oh, my goodness, Preston." I jumped up from where I sat and took a few steps in his direction. "What happened?"

His eyes narrowed in my direction. "Your boyfriend happened, Charlie. You know, my rival you've been dating in secret and were making out with at Sammi's house? Thanks for that, by the way. I really love being made a laughing-stock. It was really fun." His voice was cruel, and he reminded me too much of Anderson.

"It wasn't like that, Preston."

"You know he's my nemesis, and you've been sneaking around my back to meet with him!"

"You mean like you were sneaking around and skipping school to do that basketball training session?"

Our mom's voice came from the door of our parents' bedroom. "What are you talking about, Charlie?"

Our heads both snapped in her direction, but not before I saw the murderous look in my brother's eyes.

"Nothing," I said.

"Did you say Preston was skipping school to go to basketball training?"

I took a deep breath and nodded.

"Preston, how could you?" our mom asked, her voice anguished. "Where did you even find something like that?"

"In Denver. I wanted to beat Brooks this year. Not that it mattered, Charlie has been feeding him secrets behind my back."

My dad now interjected. "Charlie, why would you do that?"

I lifted my hands. "It wasn't even like that. We were dating, not conspiring against Preston!"

"What about that Jackson kid you went to the corn maze with?" my dad asked. "I thought you liked him."

"Wait." Preston pointed his finger at Dad. "You knew she was dating him?"

Mom spoke again. "No, honey. This was some guy named Jackson."

"And his name is Jackson Brooks." Preston's eyebrows were raised.

Mom took a seat on the couch. "Oh, my. This is getting complicated."

"It's really not." Preston forced a tight smile. "Charlie has been dating my biggest rival behind my back, you guys knew about it, I caught them making out at the party, and then he punched me in the eye. Sound about right, sis?"

My eyes narrowed. "Why did he punch you? Did you say something to him?"

He practically growled. "Because this is suddenly my

fault? Real nice, Charlie. You're my sister, you're supposed to have my back. And you're taking Brooks' side?"

I opened my mouth to say something. What, I wasn't sure. But Dad beat me to it. He stepped between us. "Enough. Your mother and I have a lot to talk about."

He turned to me first. "Charlie, you've not been completely honest with us, and you left a party in the middle of the night endangering yourself."

His head swiveled to Preston. "You skipped school and got into a fight. It's safe to say you both have made some terrible choices in the last few weeks. Consider yourselves grounded until further notice."

Preston started to grumble.

"I don't want to hear it. Now, go to your rooms. We'll talk more in the morning when we've all had a chance to cool off."

Preston and I walked down the hall. He was only a few steps in front of me, and I tried to catch him as he entered through his door. I wanted to yell at him for being such a jerk. I wanted to apologize for not telling him sooner.

But he didn't even look at me before shutting his door. The click of the lock was the only sound I heard.

I stood outside of his room for a few moments, waiting for him to open back up. I wanted to talk to him—hash things out. I thought maybe we would agree to sneak out later and shoot some hoops in the freezing weather as we talked about everything.

But he never came back to the door.

I walked to my room and did the same as Preston. I shut and locked my door. Then I turned my phone off and went to bed. I was so tired after everything that had happened, my head barely hit the pillow before I fell asleep.

CHAPTER EIGHTEEN

SCHOOL ON MONDAY was just as horrible as I imagined.

No, scratch that. It was much worse.

Preston and I had spent Sunday giving each other the silent treatment. We'd both mainly stayed in our rooms the entire day, only surfacing for an awkward family dinner. But with the start of another school week, we were forced to ride together in our shared vehicle.

We'd never been this angry with one another, and the space in the front seat was charged with our mutual animosity. Not only was he mad that I'd been seeing Jackson behind his back—which is why I'd kept it a secret, by the way. But Preston was also upset I'd ratted him out for skipping school, even though it had been unintentional.

I turned the music up in hopes of drowning out my thoughts, but Preston immediately turned it down. I turned it up once more, he turned it off.

This was turning out to be the longest fifteen minutes of my life.

I was mad about his stupid rivalry with Jackson. I'd had a lot of time to stew over it, and the more I thought about it, the more I thought the entire thing was crap! Who cared that they played against each other? It was just a high school game. It didn't mean anything in the long run.

But what *did* matter was the fact that I'd bailed on Jackson in front of everyone. I wasn't sure if that was the final straw for Jackson and I'd been too afraid to text him.

Preston had barely put our car in park in the school lot before he jumped out of the driver's seat and slammed the door. I could see him stalking toward campus through the windshield.

I texted Daria.

6:50 AM
Charlie: Are you at school yet?
Daria: 5 minutes!

I sighed and opened the text that Anderson had sent in the night. I'd been too afraid to click the link to YouTube before this moment, but I figured it might be good to know what I was up against now that I was at school. Especially since I was one-hundred-percent positive everyone at Rosemark had seen what he posted.

I clicked the link while I waited for Daria.

It was a shaky video of the scene inside Sammi's house. I was dressed in all my naughty schoolgirl glory, and

Preston had just walked in. Whoever had filmed it knew what was going to happen beforehand.

I watched the scene unfold as a fresh wave of embarrassment washed over me. The corner of the video said two-thousand views, and I couldn't imagine this could be that interesting to anyone other than those involved.

Then, the music started.

Someone had auto-tuned the entire thing. Me saying Anderson was the hottest guy in school. Anderson saying I was crazy. The whole song was frustratingly catchy, and I had a feeling this wouldn't be the last time I heard it.

I bit the inside of my cheek and looked at the parking lot, willing Daria to get here sooner. Without my best friend by my side, I wasn't going to make it. I might as well go to the alternative school now.

Thankfully, she did show up. She linked her arm in mine as we walked up to the school building.

"I'm guessing you saw the video?" she asked under her breath.

I nodded. "Anderson was so kind to send it my way, and everyone else in a ten-mile radius, I assume."

"Yeah, it's been making its rounds. It's everywhere."

"Gee, thanks," I mumbled.

"Look, I know this is easier said than done, but you need to walk through those front doors with your head held high. Don't let Anderson see he's gotten to you."

I stopped outside the front doors of Rosemark High and pulled Daria out of the way as people shuffled in. I tried to ignore the looks I got from my fellow students. "You don't get it," I said to her. "Anderson has done more than just get to me. He's won. I'm waving my big white flag."

"Oh, Charlie." My friend's brows were tipped up as she tilted her head ever so slightly.

"Don't pity me. Just let it be, okay?"

I stormed into the building wondering just how bad the day was going to be.

TURNED OUT, it was even worse than I thought.

Preston didn't sit with me at lunch, which wasn't a huge surprise. But no one other than Daria kept me company in the lunchroom. People stared and people laughed. It was like I was untouchable—and not in the super popular sense.

Even Anderson refused to look at me. I couldn't decide if I was relieved by the possibility of finally being free of him or if the radio silence was disconcerting.

But as bad as all of that was, it was basketball practice that was the hardest.

We had our first preseason game coming up, and Coach Scruggs wanted us working hard to prepare. She divided the team for a scrimmage, putting Jasmine, the team captain, on one side, and me on the other.

Daria was sorted with the opposing side. She raised her shoulders and mouthed "sorry" at me before turning and walking to the other side of the court. I watched as she made her way over to Jasmine. Instantly, her team started huddling around her to listen to what she had to say.

Coach walked over to them with a nylon bag of tacky orange pinnies. They all put them on without argument before facing Jasmine once more. I was happy they were so attentive to the team's captain, but I was feeling less confident.

I put on my brightest smile before turning and facing the girls Coach put with me. They were all talking to one another. No one looked in my direction except for one junior who rolled her eyes at me before turning to face someone else.

It was fine.

Completely okay, really.

Nothing to get discouraged by, I told myself.

So why did I feel so insecure in front of my fellow teammates? I took a deep breath, hoping it didn't sound as shaky as it felt. "Okay, so let's focus on our strengths against them."

The same girl who had just made a face said something under her breath that made two nearby teammates giggle.

Nice wasn't going to work.

It was time for my best Coach Scruggs impression. I straightened my shoulders and raised my voice. "Care to tell me what's so funny?"

But even that didn't work. No one jumped to attention. I raised my brows at the girl in question.

She defiantly crossed her arms over her chest and fixed

me with a stare. "I just said maybe you could get on your knees and beg the other team to please let us win since that seems to be your strength."

Whoa.

I knew the video was bad, but I hadn't realized how damaging it truly was. Not only had it destroyed my pride, but it had caused me to lose the respect of my teammates. How did I think I was going to help lead them when they saw me as a joke?

There was only way I could think to do it. And that was to play as well as humanly possible.

When I assigned matchups, I made sure each girl knew who to guard if we should lose the tip-off. Jessica, one of the best girls on my scrimmage team, was a split second faster than her opponent tipping the ball back in our direction. Our small forward snagged the ball.

This was the part where she was supposed to pass it to me. As point guard, it was my job to take the ball down court and call the next play, but it was like I wasn't even there. I suppressed a growl that threatened to surface as I watched her drive the ball straight to the basket, only to miss the lay-up and have the other team grab the rebound.

They quickly put the ball in the hand of their point guard, who pointed down court, setting Daria up for an easy three from her favorite spot. The ball took a hard bounce to the right, landing in the hands of a sophomore girl whose eyes nervously flicked to me before searching for someone else to pass to.

This time I did let a frustrated sound escape my mouth because it was obvious—they weren't going to let me play.

The rest of the scrimmage went like this until Jasmine's team scored once again, putting us at 45-20. They were creaming us, and Coach finally blew her whistle. She walked to the center of the court, and we all gathered around her.

"What. Was. That?" She had both of her hands on her hips. "That was one of the saddest excuses for playing I've ever seen. Charlie, your girls weren't working together at all." I felt a blush warm my cheeks. "And Jasmine, you guys might be up quite a bit, but it's only because Charlie's team was playing sloppy."

There were some quiet grumblings from some of the girls, but no one spoke up or argued against Coach.

"Now, go get showered up. I hope you will do much better at our next practice, and I absolutely expect more from you at our first game, even though it's just preseason." She lifted her hands and used air-quotes for the last word.

"Yes, Coach," a choir of voices responded.

Everyone started moving toward the locker room. I lingered and waited for each of the other girls to go ahead of me. I didn't think I wanted to hear what they were surely whispering. Thankfully, Daria also hung back.

"That was pretty rough," she said, as we finally started walking off the court.

"Tell me about it. They did not want to pass me the ball even though I am the best shot on the team. It's like they don't want to play with me."

Daria was suspiciously quiet. She was usually quick to respond with a joke or words of encouragement, so I knew something was up. I turned to her, and she refused to meet my gaze.

"What's going on?" I asked slowly, unsure if I really wanted to know.

Daria bit her bottom lip and kept her eyes facing forward. "I heard some of the girls on the team talking." She paused. "I don't think they knew I was listening, or else I doubt they would have let me hear."

This was bad, and I now knew I really didn't want to know. But I asked anyway. "What did they say?"

She stopped. "They're blacklisting you."

"What?" I shrieked.

"Shhh." Daria looked around, even though we were the only ones there. "They're pretty upset about the way you acted with Anderson. Between that and your athletic probation, they've lost faith in you, Charlie."

"Okay, but how am I supposed to get their respect back if they won't let me play?"

Daria shrugged. "I don't know, but I hope you figure it out fast. Preseason starts next week. And regular games are the week after. That means college scouts will start doing their rounds. I know you're hoping to impress them, but..."

"I might be screwed," I finished for her.

A sad smiled touched her lip. "I don't know, but I hope not."

We didn't say anything else as we got showered up and left the school. Even the ride to my house with Daria was uncomfortably quiet, and I knew it was because we were thinking the same thing.

This was bad and hoping things would magically get better wasn't going to help.

CHAPTER NINETEEN

TWO AND A HALF WEEKS.

That was how long it had been since Anderson released the video of me at Sammi's party. And while things had calmed down a little, life was still pretty unbearable.

Preston and I weren't talking, and we didn't ride to school together anymore. We alternated days with the car and, through some unspoken rule, hitched rides with our friends on our days without it. He would text me when he was going home with one of his teammates, and I'd started asking Daria to bring me to school.

With each passing day, things just got more awkward. I couldn't help but wonder if things would have been better if we just talked about it, instead of letting it get out of control the way it did.

The only time we were forced to interact was dinner-time. Our parents saw the tension between us and continued to attempt conversation around the table, but it never succeeded. Every night when we'd finished our meal, Preston booked it outside where he shot basket after basket for at least an hour—and this was on top of his regular basketball practice with the team, of course.

I knew all the extra time spent honing his skills was because Senior Year Rematch was fast approaching, and every time I thought about it, I got more nervous.

But it wasn't just my relationship with my brother. It was also my teammates. The girls still didn't respect me. The only person who gave me the time of day was Daria, and that was because she was my best friend. It had gotten so bad, even Coach pulled me aside to ask me what was going on. She'd told me if I couldn't get them to listen, she'd be forced to pick a new co-captain.

Then there was Jackson. We hadn't texted since our kiss, he hadn't shown up for Helping Hands, and I couldn't get him out of my head.

All of this was driving me crazy, and the only way I'd been able to cope was to pour myself into my studies. I was freakishly ahead on all my assignments.

I sat in my usual seat in the back of the room for Mrs. Whitmore's class. Instead of scribbling answers on the homework sheet she'd given us the night before like I would have done in weeks past, I listened as the student body president's voice blared over the speakers with that day's announcements. It was a boring list of things most students didn't care about.

"Make sure not to park in the visitor spots in front of

the office. Failure to comply will result in Saturday detention. For today's lunch, the cafeteria will be serving up
chicken patty sandwiches, baked fries, diced pears, and
your choice of milk."

"And finally, in athletic news, the boys' varsity basketball team will be playing their first game of the season
tonight at home. They're playing Pinebrook—boo—so let's
make sure to get out there and show them our support. Go,
Mountaineers!"

The school day had barely started, and my emotions
were already on high alert with the mere mention of
tonight's game. The thought of Preston and Jackson facing
off against each other caused my eyes to start watering, and
I was not about to let my classmates see me cry—not after
everything else that had happened.

I got up from my seat in the back of Mrs. Whitmore's
class, and walked to her desk. Mr. Richards' voice boomed
over the speaker as he added a few more announcements.

"I need to go to the bathroom," I said under my breath.

My teacher looked up from the lesson she was going
over. "Sure, Charlie. Just grab a pass and hurry back, so
you don't miss anything."

It was ridiculous that we were still required to carry
them around our senior year, but Mr. Richards wanted
every student in the hall accounted for.

No exceptions.

I lifted the bright yellow pass and stuck it in my back
pocket as I walked out the classroom door. Just being in the
hall, I could already breathe more easily. But I still went

straight to the bathroom, not wanting anyone to see me upset.

Once inside, I leaned against the wall and closed my eyes. As I started counting to ten, I was met with a vision of Jackson's face. Not the smiling one I'd grown so accustomed to at Helping Hands, but his face the last time I'd seen him. His expression had been full of sadness.

I hated it.

And I hated how I was more affected by a guy I barely knew than all the other guys I'd dated in high school. What did that mean for me?

I let the tears fall freely and was thankful I didn't wear makeup that morning. After a cry fest like the one I was currently having, I was sure to look like a drowned raccoon.

The squeak of the bathroom door made me go still. I hadn't even hidden in one of the stalls and was on full-display when Sammi walked in. Her perfect brown curls framing her flawless, porcelain face.

I straightened my shoulders and glared at her. With my stance, I dared her to say something—do something. Although, I hoped she didn't call my bluff. There were so many strikes against me, I didn't think I could handle one more. But Sammi didn't need to know that. She only had to see the tough girl act. An act that was a bit of a hard sell since my face was currently streaked with tears.

"Relax, Charlie. I'm not here to fight you."

My brow wrinkled. "Then, why are you here?"

She lifted her hand, complete with perfectly manicured pink nails. In it was a hall pass. "I had to pee."

I was surprised that our teacher had let us both out at once. She usually had a strict one person out of the class at a time rule. Either she wasn't paying attention to the happenings in her room—or she was paying too close of attention and thought someone needed to check up on me.

My eyes narrowed. "Why are you really here, Sammi?"

She shrugged her delicate shoulders. "Maybe I wanted to make sure you were okay."

I barked out a laugh. "That's a good one. Maybe we can exchange friendship bracelets too?"

"Fine." She placed her hand on her hip. "Do you have my jacket?"

I thought about the pink monstrosity in my locker. I'd been keeping it there waiting for the perfect opportunity to give it back to her, but Sammi was always with the other cheerleaders. I didn't want to go into the pit of vipers, especially when Linzie was around.

This was my chance.

I nodded. "Give me a minute, and I'll go get it."

I turned the faucet on and leaned over the sink. My cupped hands collected water, and I splashed my face several times to hide to evidence of my crying. Once I was satisfied, I grabbed some of the cheap paper towels from the dispenser and attempted to pat my face dry.

With a deep breath, I looked back at Sammi. She watched me with a raised eyebrow.

"Okay," I said. "Let's go."

The hallways were free of other students, and mercifully, even Mr. Richards wasn't waiting to jump out from behind a corner.

I started turning the lock as soon as we got to my locker, but I messed up my combination under the pressure of Sammi's intense gaze.

She clicked her tongue in annoyance. "We do need to get back to class eventually."

Man, I hated cheerleaders.

I swallowed hard as I tried again. This time, I popped it open without issue and grabbed Sammi's pink jacket from inside. When she reached for it, I hesitated, barely stopping myself from hugging it like a total weirdo.

This wasn't Jackson's, I reminded myself. It was pink and smelled like Sammi. But it was also a memento of that last night together. Would I ever see Jackson again? Who knew? But holding onto a tacky jacket wouldn't make that happen.

I bit the inside of my lip and took a deep breath. With a jerky motion, I shoved the jacket in Sammi's direction. "Here."

As soon as it was in her hands, I slammed my locker and started to head back to class. I'd been missing long enough and didn't want to get in trouble.

"He misses you, you know."

My feet stopped. I turned to face Sammi but didn't speak.

"Ugh. I can't believe I'm saying this." Sammi looked up and down the hall before she stepped closer to me. "We are still not friends, and if you tell anyone I said this, I'll deny it. Do you understand?"

I nodded.

"Jackson was a mess after the party. He went crazy when you disappeared, and that's why he punched Preston. For some dumb reason, he likes you, Charlie—a lot. And in some weird way, you're perfect for each other."

Perfect for each other? My heart skipped a beat.

There was an awkward pause before Sammi continued. "So, are you going to the game tonight?"

I shrugged, still utterly confused by our interaction. Sammi was right when she said we weren't friends. Probably because she was one of the cheerleaders whose hair I'd cut sophomore year. Strange how that could cause tension between people after all this time...

"You should," she said, as she looked down at her nails and let out an annoyed huff.

"And what about the whole rivalry with my brother?"

One of Sammi's perfect eyebrows arched. "Not my problem."

"Okay," I answered slowly.

"I'm going back to class. Don't come back in right after me. Circle the school or go to the nurse or something."

"But I'm not sick."

Sammi fixed me with a stare. "I don't care. I don't want to be associated with you, and you do not want to piss me off, Charlie. The only reason I'm even talking to you is because I love my cousin, and I want him to be happy."

"Thanks?"

"Whatever."

And with a flip of her hair, she was walking down the hall back toward our class. I lingered by my locker, still a little shell-shocked by everything Sammi had just said.

Jackson still liked me.

And as happy as that news made me, I still didn't know what to do about everything.

All I knew was that I needed to be at the basketball game that evening—no matter what.

CHAPTER TWENTY

"YOU'RE NOT GOING to the game tonight," my dad said, his voice firm.

"Why not?"

He lifted his brows. "Do I really need to tell why it would be a bad idea?" I didn't answer, so my dad kept talking. "Let's see. You and your brother haven't spoken in weeks because of this guy. You told your mother and me that he was a good guy, but he's constantly surrounded by drama."

"But he volunteers at Helping Hands!" I argued. "Shouldn't that balance some of this out?"

"I don't know, Charlie. That seems to be the only argument you have. And we're going with it based on his word that he isn't forced to do it like you."

Like me, but only for two more weeks. Then I was free of Helping Hands and free from athletic probation.

"Okay, so let me go for Preston then."

My dad shook his head. "If you're going to support your brother, then there will be plenty of other opportunities to do so."

"But, Dad..." My voice was whiny, and I sounded much more like a toddler trying to get out of naptime instead of a seventeen-year-old girl asking to go to a high school basketball game. What was wrong with me?

I watched as my dad's expression turned from one of exasperation to pure satisfaction. Whatever was about to come out of his mouth couldn't be good.

"How about this? You can go to the game tonight—"

"Seriously?" This was much better than I'd expected.

"—if Preston says it's okay."

I groaned. This was much worse than I'd expected.

My brother and I still weren't talking. What was I supposed to do? It's not like I could just walk into his room and say, "Hey, I know we've been fighting for weeks. But Dad said I can only go to the game tonight if you say I'm allowed. Yep, the game against the boy I like, and you hate."

No way was that happening.

"This is so unfair!" I yelled as I stomped back to my room and slammed the door. He was *my* dad, and he was totally siding with Preston. How did that make sense? I wanted to scream as I paced in the small space of my room.

I considered sneaking out, but knew Preston would see me, and I doubted he'd keep it to himself. Plus, if he had the car, how would I get to school? Walk?

Nope, I was stuck at home.

My phone buzzed, and I almost didn't check it. I was still getting random texts and messages from people at school. Most of them were horrible, and I wasn't in the mood to deal with that crap right now. But for some reason, I reached for my phone anyway.

A single text message lit up the screen. It was from my brother.

4:49 PM
Preston: You can tell dad I said yes.
Charlie: But I didn't even ask.
Preston: The walls in this house are paper thin and I heard you guys.
Charlie: Does this mean we're talking again?
Preston: I don't know yet.

Well, I'd take it for now. Although, I hoped Pres and I would sit down soon and work through everything because this talking through text messages was getting old. I sent a quick message to Daria.

4:54 PM
Charlie: Are you going to the game tonight?

She sent me three side-eye emojis before typing a response.

Daria: Obviously.

Charlie: Will you pick me up?
Daria: You're going????

What was that supposed to mean?

Charlie: Well...shouldn't I?
Daria: It'll be weird, won't it?
Charlie: Can I ride with you or not?
Daria: I'll be there at 6:45.
Charlie: Thanks! You're the best!!
Daria: I know.

I smiled at the screen, thankful for the friend who seemed to be there for me through thick and thin, even when I acted a little flaky.

Since I was completely caught up on my assignments, that meant I had way too much time on my hands to freak out about what I wore to the game that night. I had two hours before Daria would pick me up and an entire closet to go through. Before jumping into what was sure to be the most stressful task of the week, I scrolled through my old messages.

I opened the thread for Jackson and my texts. The last thing he'd sent me was "you won't have to worry about seeing me ever again." But that wasn't true. The stars kept aligning to make sure we saw each other again. First at the party, and now tonight.

The only thing left to worry about was how he would

react *when* it happened.

I SETTLED on a yellow sweater and jeans, purposefully choosing a color that wouldn't be considered cheering for either team. Preston raised his eyebrows at me as we sat down for a quick dinner, but still didn't say a word to me beyond "Charlie, pass the salt."

I wished I knew what he was thinking every time he looked at me, but he kept his expression frustratingly blank. But it was fine.

I was going to the game.

I was going to make things right.

I just wasn't exactly sure how yet.

After eating, Preston raced out the door with a "good luck," from our dad. Daria showed up at my house about twenty minutes later. She waited in the car as I said goodbye to my parents.

"I still can't believe he told you it was okay to go to the game. I was positive that was going to work," my dad said, as he shook his head.

I leaned up and kissed his cheek. "It'll be fine."

"Your mother and I hate seeing you two fight like this. I hope going to this game will somehow make things better."

I walked backward toward the front door as I shrugged at him. "Look at it this way, things can't get worse, right?"

My dad took a deep breath and released it slowly. "Have a good time, Charlie-bear."

"Thanks, Dad! Love you!"

I bounded out the front door and down the driveway to where Daria parked. Her SUV was covered in an excessive amount of shoe-polish school spirit. In green and orange, she'd written "Go Mountaineers!" on the back windshield. On one side, she'd drawn some misshapen basketballs, and on the other, she'd written: "Kill the Bears!"

Not that she was anti-wildlife or anything—just anti-Pinebrook.

Our two schools delighted in the Mountaineer/Bear rivalry. There was no doubt in my mind that we'd see "Maul the Mountaineers" on at least one vehicle in the parking lot.

"Are you seriously wearing yellow to the game?" Daria asked as I got into the passenger seat.

I shrugged as I put my seatbelt on. "What was I supposed to do?"

"Hmm. You go to Rosemark, you play for Rosemark, your brother and all your friends go to Rosemark. I kinda thought you'd be wearing orange and green." She waved a hand at her green sweater and orange party beads around her neck before she started driving toward the school.

"What about Jackson?"

"You mean the boy you haven't talked to in weeks?"

I opened my mouth to explain, but she waved her hand at me and shushed me loudly.

"Charlie, I've heard it a million times." She stopped and sighed. "Yeah, you guys kissed. And yeah, you like him. But it's not like you two were even dating. Even if you were, I'd expect you to wear your Rosemark colors."

I leaned back, enjoying the heated seats in her top-of-the-line vehicle. "Maybe you're right."

"I'm always right, silly. And I know you, which is why I also packed an extra sweater." She hitched her thumb toward the back of her vehicle.

I twisted around to look where she was pointing and saw the bright orange hoodie folded on the seat behind me. I stared at her with wide eyes. "Where did you find that?"

Daria shrugged. "Walmart. And as soon as I saw it, I knew I had to get it for you."

"Why not you?"

She managed to look in my direction long enough to raise her brows dramatically. "With this blonde hair? Don't be dumb."

The erupting laughter that came from my mouth surprised me. It had been too long since I'd joked around with Daria—or anyone for that matter. After weeks of wallowing in self-pity, I'd forgotten what it felt like to just have fun with my best friend.

And the fact that she was still by my side through my funk made me realize how great of a friend she really was.

"Thank you," I said, my voice shaking with the two words.

"Wow. Who knew tacky hoodies made you so emotional?"

"I mean for being my friend."

"Charlie, you're like a sister to me. And I know Preston already nabbed the non-blood sibling title from me—not that I'm bitter or anything," she said with mock sharpness.

"You can totally be my sister."

"Good. But I said that because I know this last month or so has been pretty horrible, and like a sister, I'm happy to support you through it."

"Which is amazing since my actual sibling is the cause of so much of it."

Daria didn't respond. Instead, she shook her head as I watched her in my peripheral.

"Spit it out," I said, knowing there was something else she wanted to say but was too afraid.

She swallowed. "Have you considered this might not be entirely Preston's fault?"

"Huh?"

"Just hear me out," she said in a rush. "I know he's got this whole thing with your Romeo, but maybe if you'd just talked to him in the very beginning, it wouldn't have been so bad."

"You mean, maybe he wouldn't have hated him as much?" I snorted. The idea was laughable.

"No. I'm not saying that. What I mean is...maybe if you'd given Pres a chance to warm up to the idea of you talking to Jackson at Helping Hands, instead of him catching you making out at Sammi's, he would have reacted differently."

"Think about it," she continued. "Your brother was all charged up after seeing Anderson humiliate you. I'm sure he already wanted to break something before he saw you kissing his enemy. Then you just ran away, and you two got grounded, and things just continued to escalate."

"But that doesn't mean he would have reacted any better if I had told him sooner," I countered, trying to refrain from pouting.

Daria lifted her shoulders as she pulled into the lot and parked next to another car decorated in anti-Pinebrook sentiments. "I guess we'll never know. It's just something I think you should consider as you deal with Preston." She paused. "And maybe Jackson."

"And what makes you think I'll be 'dealing with' Jackson?" I used air quotes as I repeated Daria's words back to her.

She smirked. "Because you insisted on coming to this game and didn't wear our school colors. Now, crawl in the back and get dressed really quickly, so we don't miss tip-off."

Her tone left no room for argument. I climbed over the center console with all the grace of a drunk sloth, and quickly changed shirts using the cover of her darkly tinted windows. Once I was done, I took a shaky breath and got ready to witness the hot mess that Senior Year Rematch was sure to be.

CHAPTER TWENTY-ONE

DARIA and I walked into the gym about five minutes before the game started. We found a seat in the stands, and I stared down at the court. Cheerleaders from both schools were going through their routines trying to get the crowds excited.

Linzie gave me a scowl as soon as she spotted me. Even in a sea of green and orange, the bright orange hoodie seemed to stand out, making me feel like a bullseye. Sammi also saw me, and a small smile touched her lips for the briefest moment. So small, I was sure I imagined it.

But I didn't focus on the cheerleaders for long. It was the players just beyond the cheer squad that had my attention.

On one side were the Rosemark Mountaineers in their green jerseys. They were taking advantage of the time before tip-off to work on some pre-game drills. From what I could tell, their coach had them doing four-corner lay-ups.

Anderson, Preston, Mackey, and Jeremiah all stood in a square. Anderson passed the ball to Pres, before running over to take his spot. Pres moved to the spot opened up by Mackey who was cutting to the basket. He got the lay-up and ran off the floor.

I watched as they moved quickly. The ball barely touched the floor as they went through the motions like they were second nature.

Soon though, my treacherous eyes found their desired destination on the other side of the court.

On it, were the Pinebrook Bears in their white jerseys with blue accents. They were also doing lay-ups but in a two-line drill. I spotted Jackson quickly. It was easy after hearing Preston complain about number eleven for hours on end.

But even if I hadn't know Jackson's jersey number, I still would have recognized him. His brown hair stuck up in several different directions, and I couldn't help but admire his toned arms on full display with his sleeveless jersey. He faced away from me as he waited in line for his chance to shoot the ball.

As if he could feel my gaze on him, Jackson looked up in the stands. His eyes immediately found mine, and we were suddenly locked in a staring contest. I wasn't sure what the emotions were behind his intense look, but I knew mine was filled with longing.

I hadn't realized just how much I missed those green eyes until now, and I willed him to smile at me, so I could see it one last time.

He didn't, but he also didn't turn away—not until one of his teammates hit him in the back with the basketball they were using.

Jackson turned toward the guy who'd pelted him, and they exchanged some words. I was way too far away to even guess at what they were saying, but a couple of his teammates looked in my direction. My cheeks heated under their scrutinizing gazes. I quickly turned my head away, but not before I recognized one of the faces.

It was the spiky blond-haired guy from the corn maze —Greyson.

"Whoa," Daria said from beside me. "That was...intense."

My face still felt warm from the blush, and I patted my hands against my cheeks. "What do you mean?"

My best friend fanned herself. "Only that your chemistry is truly palatable."

I shoved her away from me, and she giggled.

"Seriously, Charlie. The way he looked at you. That's the way every girl dreams of being looked at."

I turned my head in her direction. "Yeah?"

"Oh, yeah," she said with a knowing nod and a deep sigh.

I briefly wondered if anyone else noticed, but the sound of the announcer's voice boomed through the speakers. He asked everyone to stand for the national anthem, and soon music from a cheesy soundtrack replaced his voice. The guys from both teams stood on the court with their hands behind their backs, all facing the flag that hung on one side of the gym.

When the music stopped, the starting five from both teams stayed out there, while the rest of the teammates took the bench. Seeing both Preston and Jackson face off against each other stole my breath—and any questions for Daria that had been on the tip of my tongue only moments ago.

One of the referees stood at center court and threw the ball in the air. Pinebrook got possession, and the guy who got the ball dribbled down the court. Everyone followed, but I could only watch the way Preston stuck to Jackson. I held my breath, anxious about what would happen.

Both coaches yelled from the sidelines as Pinebrook attempted to get a basket. The ball bounced off the rim, and Mackey caught it. He drove toward the opposite basket, but my eyes continued to stay glued to Preston and Jackson.

We were barely a minute in, and they were already getting too aggressive. I watched as they elbowed one another. My hands twisted in my lap.

"Girl," Daria leaned over. "You're going to have to relax."

"But they're going to get fouled out if they're not careful!"

Almost immediately after I'd spoken the words, the ref was calling a double technical.

I turned to Daria with a smug look. "See?"

She bit her bottom lip and nodded, but we quickly directed our attention back to the court.

The game had restarted, but only long enough for the refs to blow the whistle again. This time against Jackson for excessive use of his elbow. A look passed between him and Preston. After that, the aggression didn't stop, they were just careful not to let the refs see it.

Had they silently agreed to be more cautious in their on-court fighting?

"Yikes," Daria mumbled from beside me.

"Yeah, tell me about it."

I glanced down at the bench where a few curious players from Rosemark looked up at me. Apparently, it was quite obvious to Preston's teammates why this game was going so roughly. I slumped down in my spot in the stands. It felt like everyone was staring at me.

As if reading my mind, Daria wrapped her arm around my shoulder. "Don't worry. Most people have no idea what's going on."

I nodded, and continued to watch the game, hoping she was right.

Pinebrook called a timeout, and both teams jogged over to the benches. My eyes darted back and forth between the huddles of players, as both coaches yelled at their guys like they were going to have a coronary.

I knew exactly how they felt.

When the game started back up, it was mercifully free of fouls from Jackson or Preston.

After the buzzer indicating the end of the first quarter

sounded, I could breath again. The guys had gone the rest of the time without fouling each other out. It was possible they were going to be somewhat civil to each other after getting their initial aggression out in those first few minutes.

Thank goodness.

The Rosemark cheerleaders started their routine in the short, two-minute break between quarters. Bright orange pom-poms waved through the air, and Linzie and Sammi were both hoisted above their fellow teammates. They continued to shout at the crowd to get them riled up. Everyone was cheering when the guys went back to center court.

Rosemark was up three points, but Pinebrook had possession. One of the players from Pinebrook threw the ball to Jackson, and that's when everything went downhill.

Preston went to intercept the pass and pushed Jackson hard—so hard, he ended up skidding on the court. Jackson got up, and with both hands pushed Preston back.

I jumped up in my seat as the ref finally blew the whistle.

The two were cussing and shoving each other completely ignoring the call. I couldn't make out what Jackson said to Preston over the loud roar of the crowd, but when he pointed in my direction, I knew it was about me.

It was possible I was imagining things when I felt like everyone was staring at me before, but now it was undeniable. The faces of the people next to Daria and me all turned in my direction, as well as the players on the Rosemark bench, and the cheerleaders in their orange and green. Not to mention the guys from Pinebrook who stood near to where Jackson and Preston continued in their fight, who also glared up at me.

I was sure my face was beet red under their scrutiny.

The referees kept blowing into their whistles, and teammates from both Rosemark and Pinebrook finally stepped in and broke the two guys apart.

When they were both safely on their respective benches, the referee called a time-out and walked over to the announcer's table. He said something to him, and soon the guy was speaking into the microphone in front of him.

"And that's the second double technical foul we have for number eleven, Brooks, playing for the Bears, and number three, Royce, playing for the Mountaineers. These two players will be out for the duration of the game."

The crowds on both sides of the court booed even though it was the right call. Neither had any business being on the court if they were going to act like that.

I had half a mind to tell them that and was soon given my chance.

I watched as Preston snuck out on one side of the gym, and one minute later, Jackson walked out the other. I quickly glanced around, curious if anyone else had taken notice of the coincidental absence of the two players who'd just been fouled from playing the rest of that evening's game. But no one else seemed aware, already absorbed in the game that had restarted below. Even Daria was oblivious when I told her I was going to the bathroom.

I walked out the same doors Preston had just exited. Neither he nor Jackson was anywhere to be seen, but I knew they were out there. I just needed to find them.

The halls were eerily silent as I wandered them, but I continued until I eventually heard the sound of two male voices. They were just around the next corner. My heart pounded as I crept up the edge of the hall that led to where they argued.

How had they managed to make it this far from the gym without murdering one another?

"Don't blame me because you're still sore you lost your sister at the party. It's not my fault you cared more about punishing me instead of making sure she was okay!" Jackson yelled at Preston.

"Because you were the one chasing after her? Oh, wait...you were right there with me."

Jackson said something under his breath that I couldn't quite make out, but Preston burst out with cruel laughter.

"Charlie was smart to leave you," he said.

"Why? Because you don't like me? How selfish do you have to be to let your little Senior Year Rematch dictate who she can and can't date?"

There was a pause before Preston asked quietly, "She told you what I called it?"

My breath caught at the definite feeling of betrayal in his tone. I really wished Jackson wouldn't have said that— not when Preston and I were just getting to the point where we might talk again.

"That's not all she told me," Jackson goaded.

Dang it, Jackson. Shut up!

"You'd better shut your face before I shut it for you."

Oh, crap! Not like that.

I rounded the corner and cleared my throat. Both of their faces snapped in my direction. And both Preston and Jackson had the decency to look ashamed when they saw me standing there with my arms crossed against my chest.

Before the game, I'd wondered who I would choose if forced with the decision. The idea of having to pick my brother or the guy I liked was too stressful.

But now I saw there was a third choice, a better choice.

I chose me.

I was tired of letting the outrageous competition between these two make me feel like I had to choose sides. I wasn't doing it anymore.

"You know what," I said as I shook my head. "You guys both suck. Neither of you gets to play during the Senior Year Rematch. You've let this—" I waved my finger between them. "—get in the way of the game. I bet your teammates are so mad at you, and it serves you right for being so petty."

Preston looked down at his feet while Jackson rubbed his hand over the back of his neck.

I pulled out my phone. "And I will not watch you guys fight anymore. Go back to the gym, or I will call the cops. Do you understand?"

Preston took a step forward. "You're not really going to call the—"

I started dialing.

Preston lifted his hands. "Okay, okay. I'm going."

He started walking toward the gym, and I watched him for a moment before I turned to face Jackson. He stood planted in the same place.

"I'm serious," I said, my voice shaking from the adrenaline that coursed through me. I'd never felt so powerful and so nervous at the same time. "You need to go back to the gym before anyone else notices you two walked out at the same time."

Jackson nodded his head. He started walking past me in the same direction Preston had just gone but stopped. He didn't turn around, and his voice was soft, but I swore I heard him whisper the same two words I'd been wanting to say to him for weeks before he finally walked away. The words I'd typed and deleted from my phone a hundred times.

I'm sorry.

CHAPTER TWENTY-TWO

PRESTON WAS ALREADY DRESSED and eating breakfast when I stumbled into the kitchen the next morning, my eyes still puffy from crying most of the night before. He looked up at me quickly, his face unreadable, and went back to staring at his bowl of cereal as he shoveled it into his mouth.

"Why aren't you dressed yet, Charlie?" My dad looked up at the clock on the wall. "You have to leave for school soon."

I looked down at my feet. "I was thinking I could maybe stay home today?"

"Are you sick? Here, let me get the thermometer." He opened the cabinet next to the sink and started shuffling through everything.

"No, Dad. I'm feeling fine." I cleared my throat. "I just thought I might take a much-needed mental health day."

He stopped his search for the thermometer and turned to face me, an eyebrow raised. "A mental health day?"

I bit the inside of my cheek. "Yeah."

My dad glanced over at Preston who still stared at the bowl in front of him before he looked at me. "Is this because of what happened at the game last night?"

He didn't know all the details but knew Preston and Jackson were both fouled out. And he knew I yelled at them both.

I nodded.

"Charlie." His voice was soft. "I want you to remember you are the one who begged to go."

"I know."

"Your mother and I didn't think it was a good idea, but you fought and fought until you got your way. And now you have to deal with the consequences."

I'd done nothing but deal with the consequences for these last couple of months. When was everyone else going to have to deal with the consequences? It wasn't fair that everyone else got to keep living their lives like nothing had happened, while I was dealt blow after blow.

I was sick of it.

"Please, Dad. Just this once."

"I'm sorry, Charlie, but you're going to school, and that's final. Now go get ready, so you and Preston aren't late. I'll see if I can round something up for you to eat on the way to school."

I stormed back to my room and got dressed quickly. Jeans and a long-sleeved shirt. I wanted to wear my letterman jacket—it was my favorite after all—but it didn't feel right given this past week. I settled on my hoodie, threw my hair up in a messy ponytail, and went to the bathroom to brush my teeth.

When I reemerged, it was time to race out the door. I grabbed my backpack, the granola bar my dad had left on the table, and got in the car with Preston. I was prepared to ride to school in the silence we'd had between us since the party, but as soon as we left the driveway, Preston started talking.

"You were right, you know."

I sighed. There were so many things he could be referring to, and I had no idea how to respond. I waited for him to elaborate.

"Mackey was so mad that I couldn't play last night. He said it was the reason we lost to Pinebrook."

Of all the things Preston could have said I was right about, it was the game? Ugh! Guys were so clueless sometimes.

I rolled my eyes and continued to sit there in silence.

"That's not the only thing you were right about."

"Oh, yeah?" I asked, not bothering to hide the irritation in my voice.

"Senior Year Rematch..." Preston took a deep breath.

Meanwhile, I held mine.

"You were right when you said I let my rivalry with Brooks get in the way of everything else. We went up against Pinebrook, and we lost. Life goes on. There are other teams to play. My thing with Brooks is officially over."

And so is mine, I thought. Bitterness and sadness warred with one another as I struggled to voice my reply.

"I was thinking—" Preston started.

"Look," I interrupted. "I don't want to talk about it anymore, okay? Can we just go back to our silence?"

"No."

"What do you mean—"

He slammed on his brakes in the middle of the street, cutting my question off. The sudden stop made me jerk forward in my seat. "What the—" I quickly turned to look behind us.

The roadway was clear, and once I saw we were safe from a car slamming into the back of ours, I punched Preston in the arm. "You, idiot! That could have been really bad!" I hit him again.

Preston shifted the car into park and turned on the emergency flashers. Apparently, he had no intention of moving anytime soon.

"What is wrong with you?" My voice was high-pitched.

"I'm tired of doing this, Charlie. I'm tired of fighting."

A car heading in the same direction slowed down and swerved around us but didn't stop.

"Me too," I admitted. "I hate that everything went all crazy, but I don't know how to fix it. It's like things went too far."

"Is it because of Brooks?"

My head shook back and forth. "Not entirely."

"He really likes you."

"You mean, he liked me, Pres. As in, there was a time he enjoyed hanging out with me, but not anymore." I closed my eyes and let out a sharp laugh. "And you know what the worst part is? I should have just said something sooner. Now, I get to enjoy more of these lovely consequences Mom and Dad, and Mr. Richards and everyone else wants me to learn. So yay! Lucky me."

"It's not that bad."

"Says the guy who hasn't had to deal with any."

Preston leaned back in his seat. "Everyone on the team is mad at me. I think I might have just taken Anderson's spot as the most hated player. I'm not sure if Coach will let me start at the next game. Beth is upset about the way I've been acting, and I haven't talked to my sister in weeks. I'd say I'm feeling some consequences."

It might not be as horrible as an auto-tuned video floating around the school, but it sounded like he had some issues of his own.

"That sucks," I said softly, my anger marginally less than it had been when I'd woken up this morning.

"Yeah." He inhaled a slow breath and released it. "I'm sorry about everything."

"I know."

We sat there in silence for another minute before I finally spoke up. "Um, Pres. If you don't start driving soon, we're going to be late, and I don't think that will be good for either of us."

Preston put the car back in drive, and we pulled up to the parking lot with just enough time to make it to our classes before the tardy bell rang—if we hurried.

My brother turned to me one last time before we got out of the car. "I'm glad we talked."

"Me too. But now it's time for us to run." I got out and raced to the school. Preston was right beside me the entire time until we split ways in the hall to go to our respective classes.

I skid through the door of Mrs. Whitmore's room just as the bell rang. She raised her brows at me but motioned to my seat.

My breathing was heavy as I sat down.

"I thought you were staying home today?" Daria whispered loudly from behind me.

I swiveled in my chair. "I thought I was too."

"Wait. Does that mean you rode with Preston?"

I nodded.

Mrs. Whitmore's voice called out. "Charlie, Daria, eyes up here. Class is ready to begin."

My body twisted to face our teacher, but Daria giggled and added, "That must have gone well."

AFTER SCHOOL, Daria and I were at our lockers putting our books away. We were grabbing our workout clothes when Preston jogged over.

"Hey, you ready to go?"

Daria gave me a wide-eyed look.

I nodded at her as if to say *yeah, it's weird* before I shifted my gaze to my brother and raised my brows. "Shouldn't you be making kissy faces with Beth?"

He shrugged. "She's still mad at me."

"Dude." I shook my head. "I have basketball practice, and Daria is going to bring me home. You go figure things out with your girlfriend. I promise I'm not avoiding you."

He waited.

"Seriously, go!" I gave him a playful shove that sent him in motion.

Once he was gone, I turned back to my friend and shrugged. "I guess threatening to call the cops did a number on him."

Daria linked her arm in mine as we walked toward the girls' locker room. "I think it had more to do with you standing up for yourself. It's easy for everyone to get caught up in their own drama, and sometimes you just need to let people know when they're acting selfish."

"And what about you, Daria? Do you feel like you need to kick me and tell me how selfish I've been with all this Jackson Brooks drama?"

She snorted. "Girl. Your life has been a mess, and I don't think you were being selfish—just dumb."

I playfully bumped her shoulder.

"Just remember, I fully expect you to be there for me when I go crazy."

"Yeah, right, because you're totally going to go nuts."

She wouldn't.

The thing was, Daria was crazy on the court, and you

wanted her on your team. But in real life, she was so chill. I didn't expect her ever to need me to talk her off the cliff the way she'd done for me through all my drama. Of course, if for some reason she ever did, I planned to be there with bells and whistles.

There was no way I would have survived my breakup with Anderson—or my pseudo-breakup with Jackson—without her.

We got dressed out and met our fellow teammates in the gym. Coach Scruggs stood with her clipboard looking very serious. Once everyone was ready, she spoke.

"Okay, ladies. We have our first real game tomorrow, and I'm sure you're all very excited, right?"

Everyone nodded, including me, even though I knew I wouldn't be allowed to play just yet.

"Which means this practice is an important one. We want to make sure we're really taking advantage of the time, correct?"

Again, we all nodded.

"Great. Then, let's get started."

Coach pulled out a portable speaker and hooked it up to her phone. It was odd because she never let us listen to anything during practice—not even when we were doing suicides and running back-and-forth across the court. When she pressed play on her phone, some weird new-age music, assuming you could even call it that, started playing over the speakers.

"We'll start by pairing up." She listed names in sets of two, putting me with Jessica—the same girl who had refused to pass me the ball in any of our scrimmages. A light blush touched Jessica's cheeks as she walked over to where I stood.

Good, I was glad she felt embarrassed by being paired with me. Though I was too busy trying to figure out what the heck was going on with Coach to enjoy it as much as I wanted to.

"I'm going to have you start by having the older girl catch the younger in a trust fall, and then switch places."

No one moved for a few tense seconds, but soon confused looks began to pass between everyone. The strange music played on in the background.

Coach huffed and crossed her arms over her chest. "Is there a problem here?" she asked in a loud, booming voice.

Jasmine, our fearless captain, was the first one to step forward and answer. "Um, I think we're just a little confused by why we're doing this instead of drills since our game is tomorrow." She paused, but quickly added, "Ma'am."

Coach shook her head. "You want to go through drills?"

Jasmine's eyes darted back and forth. "Yes?"

"Is it a question?"

"No, ma'am," came Jasmine's quick reply. "I think we should be doing drills to prepare."

Coach's eyes traveled over the rest of the team. "And what about the rest of you? Do you also want to work on drills?"

Everyone's heads bobbed up and down, but with noticeable hesitation.

"Then would someone like to explain to me why we've been wasting our practice time for the last few weeks?" Her question was met with silence. "No? I just figured if you're going to continue to ignore the girl who will be this team's starting point guard, once she gets off athletic probation, that you wouldn't care if we goofed around for every practice. Maybe I'll just stop showing up altogether. How does that sound?"

I winced and tipped my face down.

When no one said anything, Coach continued her tirade.

"Listen, ladies. I know you aren't all best friends, and I don't expect you to be, but your relationships out there"— she pointed to the doors that led to the rest of the school —"should never affect the way you play together on the court. You all have been acting like a bunch of overly-sensitive babies, and it's gone on long enough. I won't stand for it anymore."

The sound of a bunch of mumbled "sorry"s went through the team.

Coach lowered her brows. "I don't want your apologies. I want you to play together and beat St. Mary's tomorrow. I want to see you acting like a team. And if you ever pull this crap again, I won't hesitate to bring the incense. Then, we can all hold hands and sing *Kumbaya*. Do you understand?"

We nodded.

"Do you understand?" she repeated louder.

"Yes, ma'am," we all answered in unison.

Coach tipped her chin, apparently satisfied. Her eyes caught mine, and I swore I saw a small smile touch her lips before she started barking out orders. "Good, now get to work on your lay-ups. We have a game tomorrow."

CHAPTER TWENTY-THREE

WHEN MY FAMILY gathered for dinner that night, everything suddenly felt right again. Having Mom, Dad, Preston, and me with a giant pan of lasagna in the center of the table gave me all the warm and fuzzy feelings. It was surprising how ending a stupid argument with my brother gave me such a new perspective on meal time.

We enjoyed a friendly conversation, much to Dad's delight, and when it was all over with, I asked if it would be okay to go outside and shoot some hoops. I was still pretty jazzed up after the great practice earlier that day and wanted to spend a little more time on my ball handling.

"Wanna come too?" I asked Preston, as he piled another helping of food onto his plate.

He shoveled a bite into his mouth and nodded. "Yeah, I might come out in a little bit."

Mom and Dad's eyes went wide like we'd just sprouted

horns, or maybe halos in this instance. I guessed they were still a little in shock over the way Preston and I joked around over the meal. And really, I couldn't blame them. I was still in awe of how quickly and easily we fell back into our old ways.

Maybe that was one of the benefits of being family.

I got up and put my plate in the sink, grabbed my letterman jacket, and went outside. The evening air was so cold I could see my breath, but I knew if I moved around my driveway, I would be warm soon enough.

I spent a lot of time practicing my free throws. Sometimes, my ball would hit the rim and bounce off, but most of the time I made the basket. I loved the swishing sound when I got nothing but net. And I made a little game of seeing how many times I could get it in without it bouncing off any part of the basketball hoop.

At some point, Preston came out to tell me he had some things to do, and wouldn't be joining me, but it was okay. I let my mind wander over the events of the last few weeks, as I went through different practice drills. It felt like some awful roller coaster, and I was happy to see the end of the crazy ride in sight.

Since the auto-tuned video of me surfaced, Anderson had backed-off considerably. He got his revenge on me, and part of me thought it was even sweeter than he had planned. If that was the case, it was possible he might be satisfied for the rest of the year. So, for now, that was one problem I could check off my list.

I was thrilled Preston and I were talking again after a

stupid secret had torn us apart for weeks. He'd seemed as relieved as I was, and I hoped that it would never happen again.

Daria had taught me so much about friendship over the last couple of weeks, and I was lucky to have such a fantastic person in my life. I wished I could be half the friend she was one day.

Plus, basketball season was just around the corner, and so was the end of my athletic probation. My first game was so close I could almost taste it. I bounced the ball in front of me and took a shot at the hoop. It went right in.

Everything was looking up.

Everything except my relationship with Jackson.

The time I spent with him had been amazing. We'd had so much fun together. Jackson had made me realize what I wanted in a boyfriend. Too bad I'd completely screwed it up. I tried to convince myself it was for the best. Wasn't that what I wanted when I'd told him and my brother off the night before?

I chose me.

Then why did I miss Jackson so much?

And why did he seem like the one missing piece in my happily ever after?

I took shot after shot, working through my issues. Even though Preston never joined me, it felt good to get it all out. I wasn't sure how long I did this until I missed pretty badly and the ball went flying down the driveway.

When I went to chase after it, my heart stopped at the sight of Jackson standing there. I'd been so consumed by my thoughts I hadn't seen or heard his Jeep pull up on the street in front of my house.

He grabbed the basketball and carried it in both hands as he walked over to where I stood. I held my breath as he got closer. When he was just a couple feet away from me, he finally stopped. I wasn't sure if I was happy he kept his distance or wanted him to keep moving toward me.

We stood in silence staring at each other. Jackson's green eyes searched mine, making me feel vulnerable. My heart raced under the intensity of his stare. Maybe he could sense that in my expression because just as I was about to avert my gaze, a corner of his mouth lifted, and he tipped his chin in my direction.

"You look good in green and orange."

I snorted as I looked down at my letterman jacket. It had to be the first time anyone complemented these colors. I hated the combination, as did most people at Rosemark.

"I think you'd look pretty in anything though."

There he went complimenting me again. My mouth was tempted to curve in a smile of its own, but there were so many unanswered questions between us. I was still confused about where we stood with each other.

"What are you doing here?" I turned back toward my house, afraid Preston would see the two of us together, and I'd lose any headway I'd made with my brother.

"Charlie, don't worry about him right now."

My head snapped back to face Jackson.

"I need to talk to you." He took a step in my direction.

My heart started beating heavy in my chest as I drank

him in. "Yeah?" I squeaked. How embarrassing. I cleared my throat and tried again. "About what?"

Jackson walked closer so that he was just in front of me. The basketball that he still carried in his hands was millimeters from brushing my stomach. "I miss you."

I miss you too, I thought, but quickly shook my head. "Jackson, I can't."

His brows lowered. "What do you mean, you can't?"

I continued to shake my head. "I gotta go."

Jackson let out a heavy sigh. "No, you don't. You're just scared."

"I'm not scared," I argued, as my brain shouted liar at me over and over again. "But the thing between you and Preston. I can't let us get in the way of my relationship with my brother."

"He knows I'm here."

"What?"

"I told you not to worry about him."

"How—"

"So, we're both good shots, right?" Jackson interrupted, as he took a step back. He bounced the ball in front of him.

I nodded, unsure of why he asked and what was going on.

"I thought we might play a friendly game of HORSE."

I snorted. "What are we, twelve?"

"I'm serious." Jackson took a deep breath and turned his gorgeous eyes on me again. "Whoever wins, gets a prize. You don't need to tell me what yours is yet, but I think you know what mine will be."

I lifted my brows at him.

"I'm taking you on the second date we never got."

My heart continued to pound in my chest, even though it had been several minutes since I'd done anything but stand and stare at Jackson. I wasn't sure if I wanted to win or lose.

And what would I ask for if I won?

A big part of me wanted the same thing he did—and another part of me would just settle for another kiss like the one we shared at Sammi's party.

"Do you agree to the terms?" Jackson asked, one corner of his mouth lifting in the most adorable smirk.

I bit the inside of my cheek and nodded.

"Good." He threw the ball and, of course, it went in with no problem.

The ball bounced back to him, and he passed it to me. I walked over to where he stood and threw the ball at the hoop. It was an easy shot, and even though my hands shook a little from nerves, the ball went through the hoop smoothly. I let out a breath of relief.

So far, so good.

Jackson moved further down the driveway and sent the ball flying through the air. Again, it whooshed through the net.

And just like before, I walked over to where he stood. When I threw the ball, it bounced and circled the rim, but eventually went through. I let out a shaky breath.

It was a relatively easy shot, and I was embarrassed by how sloppily I'd thrown the ball. Jackson shot me a knowing grin, and it was so swoon-worthy, I wanted to kiss him right on the spot.

"It's almost like you want to lose," he said with a teasing tone.

His playful taunting made me relax. Why was I nervous anyway? Because some cute boy was trying to use basketball against me? And if he won, I got to go on a date with him? That was ridiculous.

I straightened my shoulders. "In your dreams."

"Every night." He winked at me.

I blushed but stood my ground.

Jackson stayed in the same place for his next shot, but lifted his left leg up off the ground, and put his left arm around his back. He balanced on one foot, and with one hand, threw the ball toward the hoop.

I narrowed my eyes at him as it went in and walked over to where he still stood. I turned and lifted my left foot and put my left arm behind my back. Just as I was about to take my shot, I felt strong hands circle my waist.

The ball fell from my hands as I turned around. Jackson's face was inches from mine. His lips were tight as he suppressed a smile.

"Are you trying to make me miss on purpose? You know that's cheating, right?"

He struggled to keep his face serious. "You were standing in the wrong spot."

I looked down at where both of my feet now touched the driveway. "No, I wasn't."

Jackson nodded. "Yep." His toe touched the ground

about a foot from where I stood. "You should have been a little further to the right."

I rolled my eyes. "You are so full of it."

"Hey." He lifted his hands. "I'm just telling you how it is. If you want to forfeit..."

"That's not happening." I stepped over one foot to the right and looked up at him. "Here?"

He nodded.

I lifted my left foot and put my left hand behind my back. I aimed and threw the ball at the hoop. It went in, and I turned around and gave Jackson a triumphant smirk.

He laughed and shook his head but moved to the next spot. This time, it was much closer to the basketball hoop, and he turned around. After looking over his shoulder and gauging the distance, he sent the ball flying. And, *shocker*, it went through.

I followed suit, and also made it.

We were too evenly matched, and things went on like this for a long time. Neither one of us missed a single shot. At this rate, we were never going to spell HORSE. In fact, I worried our poor horses would never get out the gate.

Jackson was up again and held the ball in both hands. "This has gone on long enough. I say we have an all or nothing shot."

I crossed my arms and raised my brows.

"I'm going to take one more turn. If you get it in, you automatically win. And if you miss, you lose."

"And what if you don't make the shot in the first place?" I asked.

"In the unlikely event I don't make it, you win."

I laughed. "Do you really want to take those odds?"

"It's a bet I'm willing to take."

"You're on, Romeo." My lips clamped together tightly. I hadn't meant to say it but was having so much fun competing with him, it just slipped.

A giant grin stretched out across Jackson's mouth, and I forcefully kept my eyes from looking at his lips too intently.

"Okay, Juliet. Here we go."

Jackson positioned himself so that he was directly in front of the basketball hoop. It would be a piece of cake from where he stood. I half expected him to pull out a blindfold and start spinning in circles before taking his shot.

But he didn't.

Jackson looked over at me, winked, and then threw the ball at the hoop. It hit the backboard and bounced to the left of where the hoop was. It didn't pass through the net, wasn't even close, and rolled until it was in the grass beside our driveway—far, far from where we both stood.

I stared at the ball in disbelief.

An exaggerated sigh came from Jackson. "Huh. I really thought I was going to make it."

Funny, I also thought he was going to make that shot.

I narrowed my eyes in his direction. "You cheated."

"I don't know what you're talking about." He took a step in my direction.

I moved closer to Jackson so that we were practically touching. "There's no way you didn't make that shot."

He shrugged. "My hand slipped."

"You're lying.

"Prove it." A corner of his mouth lifted.

That was it.

I couldn't fight it anymore. Caught up in the moment, I leaned into him, and put my head against his chest. I took a deep breath. "I missed you."

His arms wrapped around me. "Me too."

I drank it all in. From the familiar scent of his cologne to the quick—but steady—beat of his heart. I felt safe as Jackson's arms held me tightly against him.

I wanted to stay in his embrace forever, but eventually, he loosened his hold on me. He gazed into my eyes. "As the official winner, you still need to claim your prize."

I shook my head and smiled up at him. "I choose you."

Jackson grinned back at me before his face grew suddenly serious. His eyes searched mine, and when he'd found what he was looking for, he let out a shaky breath. He gently placed his hand on my cheek, and I held my breath as he lowered his mouth to mine.

The kiss was soft, but it was filled with promises.

I never wanted it to end—and, for a long time, it didn't.

The cold air enveloped us as we both did our best to prove who had missed the other more in the time we hadn't spoken. We put all the longing we'd experienced into that kiss, and it was a relief to finally let Jackson know how much I'd wanted him all this time.

When Jackson finally broke away, we both stood staring at each other a little dazed. I wobbled slightly on my feet though I'd never admit it.

"Wow," I breathed.

"Yeah," Jackson answered, also breathless. "So, does this mean...?"

I nodded. "I think so?"

"Oh, good." He smiled. "Because I wasn't willing to let us end in tragedy like the real Romeo and Juliet."

And neither was I.

It was impossible to know what the future held for Jackson and me, but I was confident it wouldn't involve a dagger or poison.

Sure, there would still be hurdles to overcome. Basketball season had just started, Rosemark and Pinebrook were still rivals, and while Preston had said he knew Jackson liked me, that didn't mean he was his biggest fan.

But I also knew I'd be able to work through those things, as long as I had Jackson by my side.

ACKNOWLEDGMENTS

Wow. I didn't think this book would ever get here.

Thanks be to God for letting me continue doing what I love!

And my husband and kids who keep cheering me on even after all these books. I love you guys so much!!

Jennifer and Andromeda: I have the best writing besties in the whole world. I appreciate you two so much!

Thank you, Robin, for going over this book with a fine-toothed comb.

And thanks to Angela, who caught the extra mistakes.

And Brooke. Wait. Seriously, there were more?

GG: Really???????

(Ugh, I lOve typoes. Wut wood I do without you?)

Alison: Thanks for helping me with the basketball parts so that things didn't have to stay as "SPORTS THING" in the final draft

Jessica: This cover is gorgeous. Thank you for dealing with my pestering!

There are so many amazing people in the indie community and I won't even try to thank you all. (Because I would miss someone very important!) But a huge thanks to everyone in Writing Gals and YA Contemporary Authors.

To my readers: Y'all are helping my little family every time you read one of my books, leave a review, or tell a friend. Thank you so much for sticking with me this first year and a half. It means so much to me. I adore you all!

ABOUT KAYLA

Kayla has loved to read as long as she can remember. While she started out reading spooky stories that had her hiding under her covers, she now prefers stories with a bit more kissing.

When she gets a chance to watch TV, she enjoys cheesy sci-fi and superhero shows. Most days, you'll catch her burning dinner in an attempt to cook while reading just one more chapter.

Find me online:
www.tirrellblewrites.com
kayla@tirrellblewrites.com

CPSIA information can be obtained
at www.ICGtesting.com
Printed in the USA
LVHW091217040419
612942LV00043B/10/P